The Snow Wish

By
Wendy Tackett

2 MOON PRESS
MARSHALL, MI
www.800publishing.com

The Snow Wish

Cover design by Village Graphics
PO Box 171, Homer MI 49245
VGAPMI@Gmail.com

The opinions expressed in this manuscript are solely the opinions of the author and do not represent the opinions or thoughts of the publisher. The author represents and warrants that s/he either owns or has the legal right to publish all material in this book. The characters in this book are fictional and are not intentionally meant to resemble anyone either living or dead.

ISBN-13: 978-0-9826020-4-1
ISBN-10: 0982602049

First published in 2010

10 9 8 7 6 5 4 3 2 1

Published by 2 Moon Press
307 - 1/2 West Michigan Ave, Marshall MI 49068
www.800publishing.com

PRINTED IN THE UNITED STATES OF AMERICA

DEDICATION

Thank you to my husband, Paul, and my family for encouraging me as I wrote my first novel. This book is dedicated to Brooke and Samantha.

Carpe diem!

PROLOGUE

Have you ever noticed that last bit of snow? It's the snow that just doesn't seem to melt when all of the rest of the snow has melted. I'm not talking about the big pile in the parking lot where the plows pushed all of the snow. I'm talking about the little bit of snow on your back deck or under the shadow of a big tree or on the park bench…the little bit that stays longer than all of the rest of the snow and doesn't want to melt. I didn't realize how powerful that little bit of snow was.

When I was little, I heard a tale about that last bit of snow. In the story, you had to make a guess if the last little bit of snow was going to stay until the next snowfall or melt. If you thought it was going to stay, then you should make a wish on it and it would come true when it started snowing. If you thought it was going to melt, then you should share a fear with it and your fear would melt away too. Just a child's story, right? No, it's true…and it's powerful.

CHAPTER 1

It's early November, and most of the leaves have fallen off the trees by now. I live in Michigan, so some years our winters come early and some years it's late. I think it'll be early this year. We're supposed to get snow this week, so I'm starting to do my snow day dance. I don't think we've ever had a snow day this early in the year, but I can hope. Today is the first day I'm going to wear my new scarf to school. I made it with my aunt by making knots in yarn, and I love it. Scarves are all the rage, so I know my friends are going to love it. It's definitely cold enough today to wear it, too.

Mom gave us a ride to school today since she had an early meeting. A ride is so much better than the bus! On my way to school, Mom reminded me that Aunt Leigh is picking me up after dance practice today. I go to her house every week to get some help on homework. Sometimes it helps, sometimes it doesn't. But, I always like hanging out there – we have good food and my aunt and uncle are just silly enough to be fun. They even let Marli and Leo come over sometimes too, as long as we're focused and get our homework done. Bryant, my older brother, is really smart, so he'll just go to hang out sometimes. Polly and Jason, my twin younger sibs, do okay in school, plus elementary school isn't that hard yet. I bet they'll spend a lot of time with Aunt Leigh starting next year…when they get to that dreaded middle school. Did I mention that I'm glad to be done with that? I wish Polly and Jason didn't have to go there, but I guess we all have to suffer through those years.

Ah, there he is. Leo. My boyfriend. Just seeing him brings a smile to my face. He's leaning against the trashcan by the stairs up to the front door. He's always in the area waiting for me. Even if we don't have anything to say or I don't need help carrying my books, it's just nice to see him there. I wish he could actually pick me up at home and drive me to school, but Mom doesn't like that idea yet since he just got his driver's license a few weeks ago. Sometimes I just wish we were already married. I know it's crazy to be married in high school, but life would be so much easier if I didn't have to get permission from my parents to do everything and I could just hang out with Leo instead.

"Hey, Tay. Need any help?" Leo asks as he points to my bag.

"Nah, I got it. I gotta go find Marli, though, so let's stop by the band room." Marli is my best friend, and she's so lucky that she gets to spend time with Leo in band. Marli plays trumpet, so she sits near the percussion section, which is where Leo is. Man, I wish I were in band!

Leo and I head to the band room. We hold hands for a bit, then don't. It's kinda cool. We're not the gross couple that is all into public displays of affection, but we do like to be with each other and show that we belong together. Sometimes I wish I was that girl who kissed Leo all of the time, but then better sense gets a hold of me and I realize how much trouble that could get me into at school and at home.

"Omigosh! It's awesome! I love it! You gotta show me how to make one," screeches Marli as she runs into me grabbing the ends of my scarf. "But it does cover up your necklace."

"Ya, ya. I'll show you. If you wanna come with me after school, I made it at Aunt Leigh's house. You could make one too," I said. "Besides, it only covers up my necklace when I'm outside, so I can deal with that." My Aunt Leigh and Uncle TJ gave me the necklace I wear every day. It's got a really pretty blue stone in it, and they got it when they went to Italy last year.

"That would be cool. Would she help me on my math, too? I just don't get oblique prisms," complained Marli. "You don't think she'd mind?"

"I could use some extra help, too, but I have a drum sectional after school today," moaned Leo. "We're getting ready for solo-ensemble, and I want to make sure we're as good as we think we are. Maybe I'll stop by later."

"That'll work. I wish we never had homework, though, then we could just all hang out and do whatever we wanted," I told them both.

"I could live that life," laughed Marli. "After school we could shop every day at the mall, watch every new movie as soon as it comes out, spend hours on MySpace instead of my limited ½ hour a night…that would be the life."

"Keep dreaming you two. We better get moving," suggested Leo. "You know Mr. Abrams doesn't like it when you guys are late for first block...which seems to be quite often!"

I punched Leo in the arm, grabbed Marli's arm, and we headed off to Social Studies.

Marli hung out after school at dance practice waiting for me since she's not in dance. The coach doesn't mind as long as she doesn't get in the way. We were both so hungry by the time Aunt Leigh picked us up. I wish the cafeteria were open any time we wanted food. Since we eat lunch at 10:35am, by the time 4pm rolls around – we're starving!

"Alright, I hear the tummies rumbling…do you want me to fix you something at home, or do you want to go through the drive-thru at Wendy's or Fazoli's?" asked Aunt Leigh. She always knew just what we needed without telling her.

"Can we get a frosty from Wendy's and breadsticks from Fazoli's?" I begged. "Wow, now that I think about it, wouldn't it be cool if there was a drive-thru for all the food at one place? I wish that was true. It would make things a lot easier."

"Well, until that happens, we're only going to one restaurant. I'm not going through two drive-thru lines," said Aunt Leigh.

"I vote for Wendy's, then," offered Marli. "I want a spicy chicken wrap. Yummmm…my tummy feels better just thinking about it."

It snowed a little bit during the day while we were in school, but it had already stopped snowing now. "I guess this means no snow day tomorrow," I sighed. "When I saw the big snowflakes during second block, I got excited."

"No snow day, but maybe you'll get to make a snow wish when we get to the house," said Aunt Leigh. "I don't think it's supposed to snow tomorrow, so it's the perfect time to make a wish."

"Does your aunt know that we don't really believe in that anymore?" whispered Marli. "I mean, it was cool when we were kids, but gimme a break – it's just silly now."

"I can hear you," laughed Aunt Leigh. "You never know. What would you do if your snow wish came true? It's like wishing on the first star you see at night – just something fun to do."

"I love making wishes. It's fun to dream," I said as I looked out the window at the little bits of snow in the yards as we drove down the street. "I wish everyone wanted to wear what I was wearing. I wish I had all the answers. I wish I could sing like Miley Cyrus. I wish I could meet Walt Disney. It's so much fun to dream and wish."

"My turn! My turn! I wish I were 5 foot 10 inches tall. I wish I were a model. I wish I had all of the money in the world. I wish I'd pass my math test tomorrow," rushed Marli as she took a deep breath. "I wish food would appear before me on demand. No, wait, I wish I was a genie, and then I could make my wishes come true all of the time. No, I know, I wish I was President, and then everyone would have to do what I say anyway. I'd be the first 15-year-old President. That would be so cool…can you imagine traveling to all of those other countries on a private jet and wearing the fanciest clothes around?"

"Hey, maybe I wish I was President!" I teased back to Marli. "I would love to travel all over the world, make important decisions, and do whatever I wanted. Wouldn't that be the life?"

"You two are crazy. It is fun to dream, but you need to be careful if you actually make a snow wish," said Aunt Leigh in a very ominous tone, "because it might actually come true." Then she laughed, "Okay, enough of that, let's get the food and get to work on homework!"

"So, a right prism has two side opposite of each other that are the same with right angles and an oblique prism has two sides opposite of each other that are the same without right angles," I explained. "At least that's what I think."

"You got it, girl. I knew it would eventually make sense," laughed Aunt Leigh. "Now that you girls have mastered your math assignment, what other homework do you have?"

"I have some science to do, but Tayleigh doesn't have the same class I do," said Marli. "We can work on journalism since we both have that class."

"The journalism assignment is easy," I responded. "We're both getting As in there. Aunt Leigh can help you on science, and I can start working on my social studies study guide. I just need the Mac so I can google the answers so I know they're right. Man, I wish I had my own MacBook Pro so I could just carry it around everywhere with me and use it whenever I wanted."

"Alright, go ahead and get science and social studies out. Tay, grab the Mac out of my office, and I'll go make some hot cocoa to fortify your poor, tired brains," said Aunt Leigh as she walked into the kitchen. Aunt Leigh is a consultant who works with schools, so she has an office in her home.

I started to run down the hall to Aunt Leigh's office when the doorbell rang. "Make that another hot cocoa," I yelled, "I think Leo is here." Sure enough, Leo was standing outside the front door rubbing his hands together.

"It sure is cold out there. My car wouldn't start after band practice, but I saw Bryant and he had jumper cables in his car so we got it started. Now I'm freezing," Leo chattered.

"You're just in time," I said as I kissed him quickly on the cheek. "We're just getting ready to have some hot cocoa."

"I could use a two liter bottle of hot cocoa!" Leo exclaimed.

"I wish you could have a hot cocoa IV. It would probably warm you up faster," I laughed. "But, it wouldn't taste nearly as good."

We walked back into the kitchen and sat down by Marli at the island. She was already sipping on her peppermint cocoa. As much as I like malts in the summer, nothing beats hot cocoa in the winter. Isn't it weird how it doesn't taste that good in the summer, too? And malts just don't hit the spot when it's cold outside. Bizarre.

Aunt Leigh's Hot Cocoa

6-8 ounces of milk, 1 tablespoon chocolate syrup, 2 tablespoons chocolate shavings, 1 tablespoon crushed candy cane, whipped topping

Boil the milk, but not until it burns. Add the chocolate syrup. Using a thunder stick (or blender), whip the milk and syrup into a frenzy. Add the crushed candy cane and most of the chocolate shavings – need to get them in there while it's really hot so it all melts. Pour into a mug. Add some whipped topping (we like the Redi-Whip in the spray can best), and sprinkle some chocolate shavings on top. Yum!

"Do I smell hot cocoa?" shouted Uncle TJ as he came in through the door to the garage. He had been in New York on a business trip and was just getting home. Uncle TJ is a pretty goofy guy.

He likes to joke around with us a lot and he's always sharing some strange history fact, usually about Thomas Jefferson, who he likes to claim he was named after…even though his name isn't Thomas Jefferson but his initials are TJ. I don't think I'll ever grow out of being silly right back.

"Nope, all gone, you're too late," I shouted back.

"Well, whip up a new batch then, otherwise we'll be taking a trip to White Wash City," said Uncle TJ as he walked into the kitchen. "And with so many of you here, it'll be a nice long visit."

Marli and I snickered. We knew what he was talking about, but I don't think Leo has ever visited the infamous White Wash City.

"Hey Leo," said Marli, "Maybe you can go on a little trip with Uncle TJ. You've never been there before, right?"

"The way you girls are laughing, I'm pretty sure I don't want to go there. Should I even ask? What is White Wash City?" questioned Leo.

Uncle TJ gave a huge grin, "I'd be more than happy to show you." Then he started walking towards the back door that leads to the deck. "Alright, you lucked out. I was hoping White Wash City was still on the deck, but it looks like the visit will have to wait."

"You're so lucky, Leo," I laughed. "Even though you're as tall as Uncle TJ, he'd figure out a way for you to visit. Haven't you ever heard of a white wash?" Leo shook his head no. "It's when you get your head drug through the snow without a hat or coat on. Brrrr…makes me cold just thinking about it. But, we always get more hot cocoa after the white washing. Now, talking about it, I wish there was enough snow so you could see what we mean!"

"There's no way he'd be able to drag me through the snow. Maybe he could do that to you girls, but I'm way too big," bragged Leo.

"Don't taunt him. Trust me, he'll figure out a way!" I warned. "But with just that little patch of snow left on the deck, it really wouldn't be worth it. White Wash City is best visited when there's lots of fresh snow."

"Little bit of snow?" asked Aunt Leigh. "It really does sound like perfect snow wish weather…"

"Come on Tay, let's do it," encouraged Marli as she walked over to the picture window overlooking the deck. "We made like a million wishes earlier today, so let's just make one on the snow."

"Now what are you talking about?" asked Leo. "I feel like I'm on a different planet. First White Wash City, and now snow wishes. Do you always talk in code around here? Are you guys going to turn into werewolves at the next full moon, too?"

"Hahaha. Very funny. You just haven't been here in the winter time yet. Let me educate you! Aunt Leigh used to tell me this story all of the time when I was a little kid, so Marli's heard it a million times too. It's just something fun to do," I said as I remembered being curled up by the fire as a little girl thinking everything that Aunt Leigh said had to be true.

"Don't tell the whole story," whined Marli, "That'll take too long. Just tell him what the wish is about."

"Down girl," I muttered to Marli. We moved into the living room and sat on the couch where we could still see the picture window overlooking the deck. "It's like one of those stories with seemingly normal people that something magical happens to all because of a wish. I won't tell you the whole story, but the basic idea is that the last little patch of snow that is left has magic in it."

"There's lots more snow to come this winter, so it's not like that snow on the deck is the last snow. So why would your aunt say to make a wish on it?" asked Leo.

"Hush up and let me finish," I sighed. "You can make many snow wishes during the winter. You know how it snows then melts? Well, each time it melts and there's just a little bit left, you can make a wish on that. But, there's a catch. You need to make a guess on if that last snow is going to melt before it snows again or if it'll snow before it melts."

"I know how to take the guess out of it," exclaimed Leo. "Just go to the parking lot at Wal-Mart where they plow the big pile of snow. That doesn't melt until practically June. No guessing there."

"That snow doesn't count," said Marli as she threw a pillow at Leo. "It's only the snow that is left without shoveling, snow plowing, building a snowman, or anything like that. Keep listening, there's more."

"As I was saying," clearing my throat, "now this is the tricky part. If you think the snow is going to stay until it snows again, you want to make a wish on it. If it stays, your wish comes true. If it melts, your wish doesn't come true."

"What's tricky about that?" asked Leo. "Sounds pretty straight forward to me."

"Would you quit interrupting or we'll never get to make a wish!" I shouted as I threw another pillow at Leo. "Now, let me continue. If you think the snow is going to melt before it snows again, then you want to share a fear. If the snow melts, then your fear disappears with it. If the snow doesn't melt, then you still have that fear."

"See, it's good either way. I mean, nothing bad happens. You either get a wish or you lose a fear or nothing. It's kind of like making a birthday wish or something," added Marli.

"Sounds a bit goofy," replied Leo.

"It's the goofy memories that are the best!" I exclaimed. "It's become a family tradition for us. Jason and Polly are always trying to be the first one to make a snow wish or make their wish better than the other's. Sometimes I wish they weren't so competitive, but then I guess it just wouldn't be normal. It's not like a birthday wish, either, we always say them out loud. It's just the fun of it."

"We used to be so serious about our snow wishes when we were little. We'd argue over if the snow was going to melt or not. I think the best wish I ever made was when I wished for a horse for Christmas. Tay told my parents what I wished for, and then they got me a riding lesson that spring. It wasn't as good as having my own, but it was totally awesome riding that horse!" remembered Marli.

"I remember that horse. Didn't you say it farted every other step and all the other horses and riders wouldn't come anywhere near you?" I laughed.

"Hey, I was still on a horse. It was almost the wish coming true. But ya, that was one stinky horse," chuckled Marli.

"So let's do it. Let's make snow wishes," said Leo. "I'm game. I think it sounds like fun."

"Just a minute," I said as I ran down the hall. I brought back down the MacBook Pro that I had started to go get before Leo got there.

"What, are we going to type out our snow wishes?" questioned Marli.

"No, I figured we're smarter than we were when we were five years old. Let's go to NOAA and check out the forecast," I answered smiling.

Leo laughed, "Doesn't that defeat the purpose of believing? Aren't you supposed to guess what the snow is going to do…not "know" because of what the satellites tell us?"

"You know those weather guys are always wrong," said Marli. "Just last week they predicted we were going to get 6-7 inches of snow, and we got a lousy one inch. I don't put much faith in what they say."

I googled NOAA as they were talking and found the forecast for Battle Creek, Michigan. "Well, it says it's supposed to be pretty cold – like in the 20s for the most part – for the next week," I paused. "But, it looks like the next snow isn't expected until Tuesday. That's five days away."

"There's no way that little snow on the deck is going to last until Tuesday. Even if it is cold, the sun shines on the deck and will melt it anyway," said Marli with authority.

"I'm going go to have to agree with Marli on this one," admitted Leo. "I know…there's a first time for everything!" We all cracked up. Marli usually has some pretty crazy ideas and it's rare that anyone ever agrees with her. Plus, while Marli and Leo do get along, they like to disagree with each other just for the fun of it. "Wait, do we all make a wish on the same little bit of snow or can we each find our own bit of snow?"

Marli and I looked at each other in dismay. "No one ever asked that before," I said. "I don't know. Aunt Leigh!"

Aunt Leigh walked into the living room and listened to our dilemma. "Good question, Leo. It's not part of the story at all, at least as far as I remember. I guess you could each find your own bit of snow, but I think part of the fun is watching that same little spot to see who was right," Aunt Leigh suggested.

"You'll have to let us know what happens to the snow since this is at your house," explained Marli.

"I'll text you," laughed Aunt Leigh as she walked back to the kitchen. She's always making fun of how much we text all of the time. She's not very fast with her texting, but she tries.

"So let's all wish on this same snow on the deck. It'll be easier," said Marli.

"Maybe there's a better patch of snow out there to choose. We could go outside and explore," suggested Leo.

He's such a boy! Who wants to go outside in this cold when we're inside, warm, and have hot chocolate. Marli and I looked at each other and nodded. "We're good with this snow we can see on the deck," I said.

"Yes, that we can see from inside," stressed Marli. .

"Okay, be wimps. I can deal with it," said Leo. He grabbed the computer and said, "Now I have to look at that NOAA weather report again."

“I don’t have to look at it. I know what I’m going to do. I will take the road less traveled, and it will make all the difference. Hey, isn’t that a line from some poem we read in English?” I asked. “Seriously, I’m going to make a wish. I think that snow is here to stay until it snows again.”

“Well, knowing what next week is bringing…two big tests…I’m going with the fear. And, I’m going to record our wishes on my iPhone so we’ll have video evidence! Here, take my phone,” said Marli as she shoved her iPhone at me. Then she continued with dramatic arm gestures, “Oh mighty snow, I am afraid of failing my next two tests. Please take my fear away so I can walk into those classes with confidence…and probably still fail. But, at least I’ll fail feeling good about myself.”

“You are such a loon,” I giggled as I fell to the floor. I reached over and punched Marli jokingly in the arm. “Leo, you don’t really have to do your wish in the crazy way Marli just did. Although, it would be funny seeing you do it like that too!”

“Okay,” said Leo, “I’m really nervous about solo-ensemble. I mean, we’re good, but I’m still nervous about it. My fear is that we won’t do well, so I’d like that fear to go away. If I wasn’t so nervous, then we’ll probably do even better. Do I have to say “Oh great snow” or something like that now?”

“Nope, you’re good. Your fear will be gone if the snow disappears before the next snow. That was it, you’re done. Pretty easy,” I said with authority. I handed the iPhone to Marli so she could record me. I’ve been making these snow wishes since I was a little kid. I never say a fear. I have a thing for wishes in case you couldn't tell. But, this wish is kind of different because Leo is here. Usually it's just me and my family or me and Marli. I guess I can't do my typical wishes of a fairy tale wedding or being able to fly or one of those silly things. "I know what I'll wish for – it'll be the wish to top all wishes today. I wish all of my wishes will come true!"

"You can't do that!" shouted Marli.

"Isn't that like asking a genie for three more wishes?" laughed Leo. "Doesn't it kind of go against the code of the wishes or something?"

"Well, it's my wish, and I'm sticking with it. When it comes true, you will both be jealous and want to be me," I bragged.

"Alright, I hear that the wishing is done. Time to get back to your homework," ordered Uncle TJ as he walked into the living room.

"Don't you want to know what we wished for, Uncle TJ?" I asked.

"Knowing you kids, I can pull it up on YouTube later this evening," he laughed.

"Seriously?" asked Leo. "You wouldn't dare Marli, would you?"

"The thought did cross my mind," smiled Marli mischievously.

"Gimme that iPhone!" yelled Leo as he jumped off the couch and started to chase Marli.

"She's just kidding," I yelled. "See what you started, Uncle TJ? You know we keep our snow wishes to ourselves. You totally freaked Leo out."

"Yep, and it was fun," Uncle TJ said. "Now, Aunt Leigh is waiting for you at the kitchen table, so grab your thinking caps at get back to work. I'm sure you've got some homework too, Leo, so go grab it…unless you're ready for that visit to White Wash City now…"

CHAPTER 2

I can't believe how tired I am this morning. I must not have slept well at all last night. As I got out of bed to walk to the bathroom, I noticed little snowflakes falling down outside. Phooey, not enough snow for it to be a snow day. But, it's still pretty. I know a lot of people would rather live in Hawaii or Florida all year long, but I love winter. I love making snow ice cream. I love tobogganing. I love cross-country skiing. I probably won't love it as much once I start driving, but for now there are lots of things I like about winter.

"Hurry up, Tayleigh, or you're going to be late for school," shouted my mom from downstairs. I didn't realize I'd been daydreaming so long. As least I could daydream and get ready at the same time. My personal opinion is that a hoodie and jeans with a touch of make-up works well any day. The most time I spend getting ready is straightening my hair, but luckily it was still pretty straight from yesterday. I hurried down the stairs for breakfast.

Polly and Jason were already sitting at the table eating the scrambled eggs and bacon. I sat down and grabbed a piece of bacon leaving one more on the plate. I knew the twins would start fighting over that last piece any minute, and then Mom would make some more to stop the fighting. Oddly, neither of them even seemed to notice. Maybe I really was running late and this was already the second plate of bacon.

"Tayleigh, can you come home right after school so you're here when the twins get home?" asked Dad. "We're going with Bryant to the University of Michigan to check out the housing there."

"Why are you going to U of M today? It's not like he even gets to pick a dorm until the summer, and I've heard freshmen basically get assigned to whatever is left over," I said.

"Bryant!" yelled Mom. "Get down here. We forgot to tell Tayleigh your exciting news this morning!"

I could hear Bryant making big thumping noises all the way down the stairs. Why are boys so noisy?

"The U of M admissions office called at 7am this morning, and I'm going to be part of a new early admissions program!" exclaimed Bryant. Wow, I never see him get excited over anything. He's usually pretty mellow. "Because I will have all of my core classes done this semester and have straight As in school, I'm being admitted into U of M starting in January. I'll come back for high school graduation in June, but I'll be moving to U of M in a few weeks. This is just insane! I was so sick of my senior year anyway, it's awesome!"

"What is it, April Fools' Day? I've never heard of anything like this," I said.

"It's a new program," Dad said. "There are 100 high school students being offered this opportunity from around the country, and they'll all be housed in the same dorm with some additional supportive services to help them with the transition. Bryant applied for this last summer, but I don't think any of us really thought it would happen. All of Bryant's hard work has paid off, and now he gets to be part of this. I'm not sure your mother is that excited, though."

"I thought I had another six months or so before I really had to think about Bryant growing up and moving out," confessed Mom with tears in her eyes. "I'm just going to miss him so much, but I have to admit that this is an opportunity we just can't pass by."

"I guess a lot happens when I'm a bit slow getting ready in the morning," I laughed. "Does this mean I get to move into Bryant's room after he leaves?"

"It's all yours. I'll be outta here!" promised Bryant.

I turned and looked at Jason and Polly and asked, "Aren't one of you going to try to stake claim on Bryant's room too? Actually, one of you can have my room. I'm sure you're sick of sharing a room anyway."

Jason and Polly looked at each other and both said, "I don't care." Maybe they're both getting sick. It's just not like them at all. Mom must have been thinking the same thing because she went over and felt both of their foreheads.

"Alright, I'm not sure what's going on with the two of you," said Mom, "but you're both acting a little strange. You feel okay, though, so go grab your backpacks and get ready for the bus."

I jumped up to go get my boots on so I could walk out to the bus with the twins. I admit I don't spend a lot of time with my sibs, but I like hanging out with them. Bus time is usually the only time of the day we really talk about anything.

"Wait up a minute, my phone just vibrated," I called to the twins. The text was from Aunt Leigh and read *The snow didn't melt in time. Wishes win.* I quickly texted back to her *Awesome.*

"Why don't you go ahead and call Leo to pick you up?" asked Dad. "I know you have that project to work on with Marli, so that way you can get to school a little earlier."

"Huh?" I asked. Yes, I said huh. Sounds really intelligent, doesn't it? It's not like my Dad doesn't like Leo – he really does like Leo, but he never lets Leo stop over in the morning. This is starting out to be the best day ever. I find out I'm going to get the bigger bedroom even sooner and now Leo gets to pick me up for school. Wow! Before anyone changes their mind, I grabbed my cell phone and called him to come over.

A few minutes later a horn honked in front of our house. It really was Leo. He hopped out of the car to meet me at the front door. He looked a little unraveled, which isn't like Leo at all. Leo is one of the most put together guys I know. He always looks so calm and relaxed.

"Is everything ok?" I asked him as he kissed me quickly on the cheek and grabbed my book bag.

"Hi Mr. and Mrs. Vesper! I'll drive safely and take good care of Tayleigh," Leo shouted inside the door. Then, he turned to me and whispered, "I'll tell you about it in the car. It's just a really strange day so far."

"What's going on? Are you ok?" I asked as soon as I closed the door on his car.

"I either had a really strange dream last night or I'm losing my mind," Leo explained with all seriousness. "I woke up around 3pm and felt like my arm was on fire. I jumped up and brushed at my arm, thinking something hot was on it. I felt a tube coming out of my arm, and it was really hot. I grabbed the tube and pulled it out of my arm, and it sprayed hot liquid all over me. Not just hot liquid…hot chocolate." He paused to get his thoughts together, and I snickered a little bit because I realized he obviously had a weird dream to jump start his day.

"I'm not kidding. I could smell the hot chocolate. As soon as I pulled the tube out, my arm started feeling better. It was like the hot cocoa was being pumped into my body. I took the tube downstairs and put it in the garbage in the kitchen. I even took off my comforter and threw it in the wash to get the hot cocoa out of it," he said.

"Well, now you know it was a nightmare if you were doing laundry!" I laughed.

"That's just it. This morning my comforter was back on my bed on top of me. I checked the garbage in the kitchen and it had been emptied. So, I really have no evidence that it was all real…except this," he said slowly as he pulled up the sleeve on his shirt. There was a little mark on his arm like a small puncture wound. But, it could have been from anything, so I didn't think it was any real proof.

I smiled at him and said, "It's a good story, but I don't think I'd tell people about it. They might think you're as loony as Marli!"

"It probably was just a dream," he said. "Yesterday you wished you could give me an IV of hot cocoa at your aunt and uncle's house, so I guess I was unconsciously thinking about it last night. It just gave me a weird start to my day. Then, to top it off, your parents let me take you to school when they specifically said before that I couldn't do that."

"You're having a strange day, and I'm having a great day so far," I replied. "I'm just happy that you're actually taking me to school. I mean…how great is that? My brother got accepted to some early admission program at U of M, so he's checking out dorm rooms today. That means I get his room starting after the holidays! Also, the twins were pretty agreeable this morning and didn't fight over anything. Maybe it's one of those days when things happen that you don't expect?"

The light at the intersection turned red, so Leo had to stop the car for a minute. He leaned over to me, gave me a kiss, and said, "Well, if my day is going to be kind of crazy, I'm glad you're in it to make it better." Now isn't that just about the sweetest thing? How can anyone resist that? I wish every morning started like this – it's just perfect in my book.

"I'm here for you, you know that," I offered quietly. I'm not one to get all mushy about stuff, but it really seemed like Leo was having a rough start to the day. So, I leaned over and kissed him back. Not typical me either. I don't kiss in public where people might see us. But, sometimes you need that extra kiss to make it through the day.

The light changed colors and Leo said, "We'll have to pick that up later. I think my day is getting better already!"

When we got to school, Marli was already waiting by my locker. We needed to put on the finishing touches for a project due today in Social Studies class. Marli suggested we go work on the cafeteria so we could spread out our stuff and not worry about anyone messing it up. Leo leaned it to give me another quick kiss as he headed to the band room, but I surprised everyone – including myself – by grabbing him around the neck and giving him a much longer kiss than he was expecting.

“Okay, my day is definitely getting better,” Leo acknowledged as he smiled walking away.

“What’s that all about?” asked Marli. “I thought you hated people getting all mushy in public. What’s gotten into my little Tayleigh?” Marli poked at me laughing.

“Leo is just having a bad morning, so I was trying to cheer him up a bit,” I said. Even though that was the truth, I had to admit it was kind of fun doing a few things outside of my comfort zone for a change. I then filled Marli in on Leo’s morning hot cocoa adventures.

“Mmmm…hot cocoa. That sounds good,” she said.

“All you think about is food. Did you even hear the rest of the story?” I asked while laughing.

“Speaking of hot cocoa, though, look over there!” exclaimed Marli as she pointed to the cafeteria line. “It’s open! The café is never open in the morning. I’m going to go see if they have any hot cocoa.” She ran up to the counter. Sure enough, a few minutes later she came back with two hot cocoas in her hands.

“Mrs. Appleton thought it would be interesting to see if kids will actually buy things at the café in the morning. She said that she noticed a lot of kids hanging out in the cafeteria before school and in between classes, so she’s going to have it open for a while as a test.

She'll have different things available throughout the day, so we can even grab a snack in between classes. Probably just another way for the school to make money, but it's all good with me!" explained Marli.

"Too bad Leo missed this, I'm sure he would have thrown up if you'd brought him some hot cocoa," I said as we both dissolved into laughter. Hot cocoa in hand, we finished up our work on the class project and made it just in time before the bell rang.

As we were walking to our Social Studies class, I saw Vanessa start to walk towards us. "Oh great, here comes the uber snob," I whispered to Marli.

"What rude thing do you think she'll say to us today? Is my hair too messy? Are my eyelashes stuck together? Should I get a botox injection? Man, she just makes me sick. Like she's so perfect. Not!" said Marli in a voice that was a little too loud for my comfort. I was worried that Vanessa would hear her, and then she'd be even meaner to us.

"Taaaaaaayleeeeeeeeee," Vanessa whined in her sickly sweet and slow voice. "Where ever did you get that hoodie? I must have one too."

I was waiting for the punch line. Waiting for Vanessa to say something like how only people who go dumpster diving would wear this hoodie.

"Leave me alone, Vanessa. We have to get to class to turn in this project," I quickly said.

"I'm serious. I love that hoodie. If you won't tell me where you got it, I'll figure it out myself," she huffed as she turned and walked away from us.

"Was that bizarre or what? I think she was actually trying to be nice," I said to Marli.

"Nah, it's her new technique. I'm still on guard. I have no idea where she's going with this one," replied Marli.

We continued down the hall to class. Just before we walked into our classroom, Alex shouted across the hall to me, "Hey Tay, where'd you get your jeans? I want to buy a pair like that for my sister for her birthday."

Me giving fashion advice? What was going on? No one ever comments on what I wear or cares what I wear. Maybe Vanessa talked to Alex and got him to ask that, although I don't think they're really friends. I don't think Vanessa is really friends with anyone.

"Gimme a break, Alex," I hollered back at him. But, what if he really was asking because he wanted them for his sister? Was I just rude to him? Alex always seems to be pretty nice to me. I hope I wasn't just rude. Now I'm going to worry about that until I see him next. I wish I'd just answered him and not overanalyzed it all. Really I wish Vanessa would just leave me alone. She stresses me out. She's a major source of the drama that is high school…the part of high school I really don't like at all.

At least turning in our Social Studies project was a lot easier than I thought it would be. Mr. Abrams is famous for deciding on the spur of the moment to make us do presentations, so I was expecting something like that. Not that Marli and I actually prepared for it, but I still figured it would happen. Instead, Mr. Abrams said he realized he'd been working us all pretty hard lately so he wasn't going to assign any more homework until after Christmas break. That's like four weeks away. Four weeks of no homework…yeah! For a minute there I thought he was going soft on us, but then he explained what was really going on. Because we're all going to be taking some new national standardized tests in various classes over the next few weeks, all of the teachers agreed that is stressful enough so they're not going to assign us any homework until the new year. I'm good with that. I don't care what the reason is. No homework is always a good thing!

After Social Studies I headed to choir. Choir is always my favorite class of the day. I've never had to sing a solo, so I just get to have fun in class...no pressure. I'm in there with a lot of my friends, so we always try to make time to catch up on what's going on. I like our new choir director, Ms. Planter. She's younger than most of my teachers, so we feel like she can relate better to us. I also really like the songs we're singing now because they're all Christmas arrangements. Some of the songs we sing at other times of the year aren't as fun because nobody knows them at our concerts, but everyone knows Christmas songs even if we do sing them a little differently. We're doing *Here Comes Suzy Snowflake* this year, which was one of my favorite songs as a kid. Not a typical traditional Christmas song, but still fun.

"Tayleigh, I'm been wanting to talk to you," said Ms. Planter as I walked into the choir room. "First of all, though, I have to say that I really like your outfit today. Very well put together. Anyway, didn't you say that you were Suzy Snowflake in 1st grade during a Christmas show?"

"Yes, but thankfully there's no video evidence of that," I laughed. Did a teacher just comment on my outfit? A hoodie and jeans – nothing special about that. That's the third person today that has said something about what I'm wearing, and I've probably worn this same outfit like three or four times in the last month. Oops, here I am obsessing about my clothing now and not even paying attention to what Ms. Planter is saying.

"…so, do you want to try it? I know you're not one that typically wants to do solos, but I thought you might enjoy it since it's a special song for you," said Ms. Planter.

"Ummmm…what?" I asked, looking pretty confused I'm sure.

"Do you want to try out for the Suzy Snowflake solo?" repeated Ms. Planter.

What is she thinking? Seriously? What if I pass out? I love singing in the choir, but I don't know about singing by myself. "I don't think so," I meekly replied.

"Why don't you try it today in class and we'll see how it goes. If you're really not comfortable with it, I can ask Erica or Sabrina to do it. But, I have a feeling that you'll do just fine," encouraged Ms. Planter.

I just nodded. How can I say no to that? At least she's letting me try it out in class first where the worst I can do is embarrass myself in front of all of my friends. Oh crap, now I'm getting nervous. What does Uncle TJ always tell me to do? Breathe slowly and let the nervous energy out …ya, that's it. UGH! I wish I wasn't doing this.

We started singing the song. I knew where I was supposed to sing the solo, and thankfully Ms. Planter wasn't making me stand in front of the class or anything. Okay, here it goes, "Come out everyone and play with me, I haven't long to stay. If you want to build a snowman…" My voice dwindled off as I realized everyone was staring at me. OMIGOSH! I must be horrible. I'm so bad they all stopped singing. Why did I agree to this? I wish I'd stayed home sick today. I think Leo's bad day is rubbing off on me.

"Tayleigh, where have you been hiding that voice?" demanded Sabrina.

"That was amazing!" shouted Erica, with others agreeing.

"I think we have our very own Miley Cyrus here," said Ms. Planter. "Now we just have to help you with some confidence so you can perform like Hannah Montana." She walked up and gave me a big hug. Okay, now I'm totally confused. Was I really that good or are they making fun of me? They have to be making fun of me. I remember when I was little, people at church would tell me I had the loudest voice in the choir. I thought that meant the best voice, and I was so proud. Then one day I realized it just meant I was the loudest, not the best.

"Alright, stop it already. I know it was bad, but you don't have to keep making fun of me like that," I said as my lip started to tremble. I was NOT going to cry in front of everyone. I'm so embarrassed.

Ms. Planter was standing right next to me and put her hands on my shoulders, turning me to look at her. "I'm not kidding with you, Tayleigh. Your voice surprised us all. You've been hiding your talent from us. We've just never heard you sing like that before."

"Seriously, I thought you had a recording of Miley you were playing through your iPhone or something," said Sabrina. "You sounded just like her."

"You know," said Ms. Planter, "I have an idea for something that you may be just perfect for, but I can't tell you just yet. Let me think about it a little more, and then I'll let you know. But let me just say that I think the band director is going to be very excited about your voice, too."

"Okay, you guys are freaking me out now. Can we get back to singing?" I asked. I'd much rather have the attention elsewhere. I was getting even more nervous with everyone fawning all over me. I'm just a choir member. I'm not a soloist. I wish they'd all look at someone else.

I just kind of floated through the rest of the day. My nerves were shot after choir. I don't like being the center of attention like that at all. I'm not sure what was going on, either. I've always liked to sing, but I've never been the best singer. It would be so cool if I really can sing a solo at the concert. My parents would be so proud of me. The day really does go quickly when I don't pay close attention. I hope I didn't miss too much. I guess it doesn't matter since we don't have homework anyway. Yeah about that!

"I really wanted to go to the mall," pleaded Marli. "Are you sure you can't go tonight?"

"Dad asked me to go right home after school to watch the twins. I know they're old enough to be home alone, but Mom and Dad are taking Bryant to U of M this afternoon. Since they'll be out of town, they want me home," I responded.

"I guess I understand," sighed Marli. "We really do need to go to the mall soon so we can pick out dresses for the Winter Carnival. You don't want Leo to have his date go in some re-used middle school dress, do you?"

"We have well over a week before the dance. There's still plenty of time. If we don't get there in the next few days, we'll definitely go this weekend. But hey, with no homework, that means we'll have lots of free time in the evenings!" I exclaimed.

"Well, if we're not going to the mall, can I hang out at your house?" Marli asked.

"Like you even have to ask? Duh. You practically live at my house anyway. You can help me practice my singing," I said.

"I have to listen to that screeching?" laughed Marli. "Maybe I'll just hang out with Jason and Polly."

Thankfully Leo gave us a ride to the house so we didn't have to take the long bus ride home. Bryant takes us home most days, but obviously he was with Mom and Dad today. With Bryant leaving for U of M, my built in ride will be gone. Hmm, I hadn't realized there would be bad side effects from Bryant's leaving.

CHAPTER 3

Today isn't much different from yesterday so far. People keep coming up to me and congratulating me on my singing or complimenting me on my outfit. It's just so bizarre. I wish Marli, Leo, and I could just escape somewhere far away…especially far away from Alex. I still find it hard to believe he wants to buy my jeans for his sister. I'm sure Vanessa is involved in this somehow, but I haven't figured out her angle yet.

Journalism. Finally. I have an article I'm working on. It's about Walt Disney. He's one of my favorite people ever. I'm writing a story about his vision and sense of imagination and how we can all use a little of that in our daily lives. I know Disney so well, the article can almost write itself. I can fade into the background. I have to do a little research on the computer, but I don't havc to interview anyone or be in the front of the class or anything. I need a little anonymity now.

I walked into journalism and saw Leo. It's the one class we have together because students from 9th-12th grades are all in the same class. In order to get into this class you have to write an essay in the summer explaining why you think you should work on the school newspaper, and you have to submit a sample article that you've written. I've always liked to write, and I do our family's newsletter every Christmas, so I thought this class was a perfect fit for me. It just makes it extra cool that I get to have this class with Leo. I walked over to him and gave him a quick kiss, which got a lot of looks from other kids in the class because I don't normally do that.

"Alright, the bell has rung, that means we need to settle down and get started," said Mrs. Kipp. Since choir and journalism are at the opposite ends of the building, I never get to class with any extra time left. "I have an exciting announcement to make."

"We already know about the no homework through the new year, but we'll act excited when you say it again," said Keith, who can sometimes be a smart aleck. "Because I really am super excited about it!"

"I'm sure that was exciting news for all of you, but that's not it," paused Mrs. Kipp. "The owner of the radio station WBCK has been reading the high school newspapers throughout the county this year. The schools were not aware of this, but WBCK was running a secret contest. They were looking for the school newspaper that best covers local news in an unbiased way. So yes, Vanessa, that means they weren't looking at the editorials. Sorry."

Everyone laughed. Vanessa's editorial section was like a checkout lane gossip rag, but everyone did read it. A lot of people get mad at her for what she writes, but it's still the most popular section of our paper. Kids can be so mean sometimes.

"Anyway, our newspaper won their competition!" announced Mrs. Kipp with great enthusiasm that was met with a lot of blank stares from the class.

"So, what's that mean for us?" asked Bill, an eleventh grader.

"It means that they will be printing one column of our choice on their web site and also reading it on air every week for the rest of the school year. The student who writes the column each week will get to go to WBCK and read it live on air," shared Mrs. Kipp, "which I think is pretty exciting and great exposure!"

"How will we decide which column gets picked each week? If it's the headline each week, that's not fair because the same few people write the main stories all of the time," cried Morgan.

"Good point," accepted Mrs. Kipp. "That's why I thought I'd pick a name out of a hat each week and that person's column will be the one used. Once your name has been picked, it won't be picked again. There's just enough weeks for everyone's name to be picked, so you each will have this excellent opportunity to be published on the web and talk on air."

"Even me?" asked Vanessa.

"They didn't count your column in the contest, but we'll include you for the weekly drawing. However, I will have final editing rights to anything that is read on air, Vanessa," said Mrs. Kipp as she gave Vanessa one of those looks. "And those of you who work on advertising will get to go on air at some point, too, we just need to figure out how that will work since you won't be reading a column. Maybe we'll give some free on air advertising to some of our sponsors. Free…oh, that reminds me. There's something else that goes along with this. WBCK also gave our class three brand new MacBook Pro computers for our classroom…and three more to give out to students in class! We're going to have a drawing to see who wins their own laptop computer."

The class dissolved into hoots, hollers, and questions at that announcement. Didn't I just wish the other day that I could have my own laptop? This would be just great if it came true! I'm not the luckiest person in the world, though. I rarely win anything.

"Calm down! Calm down," shouted Mrs. Kipp. "I have everyone's name in this box, and I am going to draw out three names. Please no fighting or arguing. We just need to be happy for those who win these computers. Hopefully the computers will be used to write even more articles for the newspaper. We'll all get to use the new computers in the classroom, so it's a win all around. Okay, the first new laptop owner is…Jeremy!"

Jeremy stood up and took a bow with everyone clapping. He's a really nice guy, and I know for a fact that he often comes to the computer lab after school to do work so I don't think he has a computer of his own. I can be happy for him. Now, I wish Mrs. Kipp would call me next. Call me next. Call me next. Come on Mrs. Kipp, just say my name. You can do it.

"The next new laptop owner is…Tayleigh!" exclaimed Mrs. Kipp.

I started clapping with everyone else until Leo hit my arm. "Didn't you hear her, Tay? She said your name!" yelled Leo in my ear.

No way! Seriously? Me? Wow, my wish came true. I wished for it the other day, and it came true today. I kept talking to myself in my head so I didn't actually hear Mrs. Kipp say my name. This is the coolest thing ever. I didn't even hear who else got a computer because my brain was in a fuzz for the rest of the hour. I just kept thinking over and over again that my wish came true and I have my own MacBook Pro. I wonder if this is because of my snow wish. I wished that all of my wishes would come true, and one just did. Did my snow wish really work? I couldn't wait to take it over to Uncle TJ's house. He's a Mac genius and would hook me up with all of the coolest software. Then I can also ask Aunt Leigh about my snow wish.

"The new laptop owners can pick up their computers at the end of class, but now we need to focus on writing some articles for this week's newspaper," announced Mrs. Kipp.

"Is this like the best couple of days ever?" I quietly squealed to Marli and Leo at lunch. "I am a proud MacBook Pro owner!"

"Don't forget about the no homework deal now. That's a big one for all of us," added Marli.

"Right. Right. How could I forget that? It just seems like everything is going my way," I said as I smiled dreamily.

"Your way. Not mine," reminded Leo. "You didn't wake up yesterday at 3am with an IV of hot cocoa sticking out of your arm."

"It was a nightmare, Leo, but I agree you didn't have the best start yesterday. It's gotten better, though, hasn't it?" I asked as I kissed him.

"Again, Tay? You're getting to be like one of *those* couples," Marli complained as she pointed to the table in the far corner where some of the girls in school that we don't talk to hang all over their boyfriends throughout the entire lunch period.

"Oh gross!" I howled. "Please hit me if I become one of those!"

"I'm close to hitting you, then," laughed Marli.

"I doubt that'll really happen," said Brittany as she walked by our table. "There's no way they'd close school in the middle of the day."

"What did she just say?" asked Marli. "I swear Brittany just said something about school closing. I'm going to go find out." She jumped up from our table and ran over to Brittany. Marli is always the first one to text me in the morning if school is closed. I think she lives for unexpected days off of school. Way back in 5th grade something with the electric company blew up near our school so we lost electricity for two days and didn't have school. It was in the spring, too, so it was perfect weather for hanging outside and having fun. You have to enjoy those days when you can. Marli and I had so much fun just being kids with no rules and no responsibilities. Although now, I usually just go back to sleep on snow days and sleep until noon!

"Want to go to Best Buy after school today to see if we can find a cool laptop bag for your new MacBook Pro?" asked Leo.

"Great idea! I'll text Mom and let her know where we'll be. I'm sure she won't mind once she hears I have a new laptop. And, with no homework tonight, she can't insist I come home to work on it!" I replied gleefully.

"The rumors are true. They're thinking about cancelling school early today," rushed Marli as she got back to the table.

"Why?" Leo and I both asked at the same time.

"Have you looked outside lately? It's been snowing like crazy since sometime during 2nd block. I guess it's supposed to keep snowing like this for a while, so they don't want everyone on the roads later when it's even worse," replied Marli.

"Do you know when they're going to announce if school is closed early?" Leo asked.

"I guess there's some problem with the buses right now. If they can figure all that out, they'll let us go early. You know, they have to get all of the elementary and middle school kids too. I'm sure they'll make an announcement when it's all figured out," Marli said.

"If we do get out early, we can get the laptop bag then head over to Uncle TJ's so he can start getting me hooked up with all of the good stuff on the Mac!" I suggested. "I gotta talk to Aunt Leigh about my snow wish, too. I'm starting to think it might actually have come true. I mean, I wished to win that laptop, and I did. Maybe it really is connected."

"Make another wish and let's see if it comes true. If it does, then we'll know your snow wish was for real," suggested Marli.

I was just about to make a wish, but the school intercom crackled as an announcement started,

"ATTENTION ALL STUDENTS. SCHOOL IS CLOSING EARLY DUE TO DANGEROUS ROAD CONDITIONS. THE BUSES WILL BE HERE TO PICK UP STUDENTS IN 15 MINUTES. STUDENTS WHO DROVE ARE FREE TO LEAVE NOW. NO STUDENT MAY WALK HOME. IF YOU NEED TO ARRANGE TRANSPORTATION, PLEASE COME TO THE OFFICE OR USE THE PHONE IN YOUR CLASSROOM. PLEASE BE SAFE AS YOU TRAVEL OUT INTO THIS SNOWSTORM."

"I'll text my folks to let them know I'm getting a ride with you and Leo," said Marli. "That's okay, right?"

“Sure thing. I just want to get where we’re going soon. I don’t have the best snow tires on my car,” explained Leo.

“Wow, what a crazy day! We have no homework tonight, school is out early, no dance practice…I won’t know what to do with myself,” I commented as we walked to our lockers.

“More time to play with the new MacBook!” squealed Marli. “I feel like I won a computer because you know I’m going to be using it all of the time to check MySpace and FaceBook!”

“I still can’t believe I got that. One of my wishes actually came true,” I smiled.

“Hey, that reminds me, have any other wishes come true for you since the snow wish?” asked Marli.

“No, the computer thing came true, but that’s just one thing. I also wished yesterday that Vanessa would stop bothering me, but she’s still around and as annoying as ever. So, that one didn’t come true. I would definitely say *all* of my wishes aren’t coming true,” I said with confidence.

“Well, it’s still cool that one wish came true. It’s a pretty big one, too,” reminded Marli.

“Yep, I can’t complain,” I replied. “Let’s hurry up and run to Best Buy.” I threw my arm around Leo, carefully transitioning the laptop to his arms while I got my coat out of my locker. “No books to take home…yeah!” I shouted.

"Did you text your mom yet? It is okay to run to Best Buy then to your uncle's house?" asked Leo.

"Sure thing – I can multi-task. She said it was fine, as long as the roads were okay. But, since Best Buy is on the way to Uncle TJ's house, she can't really complain about that. And, if worse comes to worse, we stay there. Aunt Leigh loves to entertain, and they have extra beds," I commented.

"And Leo can get his white wash now that there's enough snow," added Marli.

"Maybe I'll just drop you ladies off," laughed Leo.

"I'm glad I'm not traveling this week," confessed Uncle TJ. "You know I love to be around for the birth of a new Mac user!"

"I've been using your Macs for years, Uncle. I'm hardly a new Mac user," I whined.

"Okay, okay. A new Mac owner, then. This is the first Mac of your own," he explained.

"True that!" shouted Marli. "I'm kind of thinking it's like my Mac, too. I can pretend, right?"

"Let me get the camera. We'll have to take pictures of you unpacking the laptop and using it for the first time," explained Aunt Leigh. "You know how silly your uncle gets about this. It's a whole production."

"Which is exactly why I wanted to come here," I said. "It's a pretty big deal, and I knew you guys would understand and help me get it set up."

"With hot cocoa to toast the new computer," chimed in Marli. "And enough snow for a white wash for Leo!"

"Is this the point where I should leave now?" threatened Leo.

"Hey, wait a minute, didn't you wish for enough snow so Leo could get a white wash? That wish came true, too!" exclaimed Marli.

"Yes, but I wished for that before the snow wish would have taken effect. My wishes after the snow wish are the ones that should come true," I said matter-of-factly. "Here, let me try it out. I wish for a one hundred dollar bill to appear in my hand now."

Nothing happened. "Maybe you need to wave your hands around. You make fun of my dramatics, but you underestimate the inspiration in dramatics," said Marli.

I turned to look at her, and when I looked back at my hand there was a piece of paper there that read:

Bill for $100. Payable to Uncle TJ.

"Very funny, Uncle TJ," I muttered as we all cracked up. "I only pay for computer help with hugs."

"I suppose that'll work," said Uncle TJ as he put his arm around me. "Now, let's take some pictures and load some software."

Aunt Leigh took like a million pictures of me opening the computer, standing by the computer, standing with Marli and Leo, turning the computer on, loading software with Uncle TJ, and even making a toast with the hot cocoa. She's a little picture happy, but I must admit it is fun looking back at pictures taken over the years. I look pretty darn cute in most of them! I already told her she has to help plan my graduation party from high school – I'll be the one with the most pictures ever. She's probably have to help out with Marli's too since she has hundreds of pictures with the two of us together.

Before we knew it, it was time for dinner. We'd been here for hours working on the computer. It was a lot of fun, though, and everyone got a chance to play. We even video chatted between Aunt Leigh's computer, Uncle TJ's computer, and my computer. How cool is that?

"I'm hungry," complained Marli.

"You're always hungry," I retorted. "But, I guess I'm a little hungry, too. You know what sounds good? A hot baked potato with cheddar cheese and broccoli."

"Fettuccine alfredo with cheesy garlic bread," added Marli.

"A bacon cheeseburger with chili cheese fries," offered Leo.

"Well I know I definitely don't have the ingredients to make all of that," said Aunt Leigh.

"It looks like the snow has let up some outside," noticed Uncle TJ. "We could take the Jeep out and try that new restaurant."

"What new restaurant?" asked Marli. "How can there be a new restaurant and I don't know about it? Did Olive Garden finally open here?"

"There was an article about it today in the newspaper," responded Aunt Leigh. "It's only a drive-thru restaurant, and it's supposed to have a huge menu…pretty much anything you could want."

Marli and I looked at each other, our jaws dropping open. "You're making fun of us, aren't you?" asked Marli.

"The article is right here," said Uncle TJ as he brought up the newspaper's web site on my computer. "It's near the mall, so it's not far away."

"We were just wishing for a drive-thru restaurant with all types of food!" I exclaimed.

"It's just one of those days when everything goes right for you, isn't it?" joked Leo.

"Everyone in the Jeep," ordered Uncle TJ. "Let's go!"

"Tell you what, after dinner we can come back here and make snow ice cream. With all of this fresh snow, it's the perfect time to do that," suggested Aunt Leigh.

"Is your family obsessed with snow?" laughed Leo. "White Wash City, snow wishes, and snow ice cream…very weird."

Marli and I looked at each other and cracked up. I guess it is true, we do have some silly traditions during the winter, but it makes the dark winter days a lot more fun.

Snow Ice Cream

1 large bowl of clean snow, 1 cup sugar, 1 egg, ¾ cup evaporated milk, 1 teaspoon vanilla, assorted toppings

Whip the sugar, egg, milk, and vanilla together. Add snow little by little until your ice cream has the consistency you want. Decorate with chocolate chips, sprinkles, nuts, caramel, and whatever other goodies you have!

Dinner was awesome, and so was the snow ice cream. I put some chocolate syrup on mine along with some peanuts – yum! After we pigged out, Leo took me home and I got to show off my new computer to everyone. Bryant took a special interest in it, claiming I should give it to him.

"College students all have laptops, so I'd make really good use of it. You know there's no way I'm getting a laptop otherwise. You should let me take it to U of M," nagged Bryant.

"In your dreams," I snickered. "I might let you use it when you visit home, but only if you're nice to me."

Polly and Jason didn't seem too interested. They were both sitting in the living room watching a TV show without arguing over the station.

"Are you sure nothing is wrong with the twins?" I asked Mom.

"I know, they're not acting like themselves at all. I figured as soon as they got home they would be outside seeing who could build the bigger snowman or who could sled down the hill on the side of the house faster. I'm not sure what's going on with them," Mom replied.

"I'm surprised they're not clamoring over your computer, Tay. I'm sure they're both dying to check their MySpace accounts, but they're acting like they don't even care about it," said Dad.

"Well, since I have dance practice after school tomorrow, maybe I'll leave the laptop at home so they can play with it after school. Not that I'll always do that, but maybe it'll help get them out of their funk," I offered. "That's *if* we even have school tomorrow."

"That's very nice of you, Tayleigh. I'm not sure I like the idea of you taking it to school anyway," said Mom.

"I want to take it to school, and I'll take good care of it. That's why we got the laptop bag. My journalism teacher said I could use this computer in class, too. I bet some other teachers will let me use it in class," I said. It's my computer. Mom can't tell me what I can and can't do with it. Well, I guess she can, she is my mom. But I really would take good care of it.

"We'll talk about this later," acknowledged Dad. "You all need to get to bed. The snow has stopped and the plows came through, so I'm sure you'll have school tomorrow. It's late, so everyone up to bed."

"Ah, Dad," I complained, looking over at the twins expecting them to join in with me. Nothing. Jason turned off the TV, they hugged Mom and Dad, and headed upstairs. Did zombies replace the twins without any of us realizing it? Great, now I've scared myself and I know I'm going to have nightmares!

CHAPTER 4

So far today has been more of the same weirdness. I've had several people come up to me and tell me my outfit today is cute. I can understand people saying that if I have on some hot sweater or new skirt, but I'm wearing jeans and a hoodie again. It is my sage green hoodie, which is pretty sweet, but anyone can go buy at it Aeropostale. It's too cold out to be stylish, I'd rather be warm. And, I sang well again in choir. I think I am actually going to have to sing the solo in public. I hope I don't faint when the concert happens. Thankfully it's a few weeks away yet – plenty of time for me to get even more nervous.

The weirdest things so far today all happened in journalism class. Mrs. Kipp asked why I didn't bring my new laptop to class to use, so I explained how I left it home for the twins to use after school. She said I should carry it around with me always in case I need it, and she called my Dad at work! Seriously. What was she thinking? Dad left work, went home, got my laptop, and brought it to me halfway through journalism class. First of all – embarrassing. Second of all – I really didn't need it. Just something extra to carry around with me now.

Before Dad got there, I was doing some research on my Walt Disney article on one of the school computers, and then I continued working on it on my MacBook Pro. I found that there's a boy named Walt Disney who lives in Marshall, which is only like 15 minutes away. I wonder if he's related to the real Walt Disney. I've never heard of anyone named Disney before. He must be related. This is so cool. I wasn't going to do an interview as part of my article, but this could be a real human interest piece now.

"Can you call Marshall Junior High to see if I can interview Walt? He's in 7th grade over there. I'm sure he'll think I'm crazy if I call out of the blue, so maybe you can talk to his teacher first," I suggested to Mrs. Kipp.

"You're the journalist. I'm not going to do your work for you. If you run into any problems, then I'll help out, but you need to try it yourself first," explained Mrs. Kipp.

"Can I at least use the phone in here so the school can see it's another school calling?" I asked.

"Yes, go ahead. Just be honest and explain who you are, where you're from, and why you want to interview this student," Mrs. Kipp guided. "You may even find out that's not his name – you can't trust everything you find on Google."

I went ahead and called over to Marshall Junior High. I got to talk to Walt's homeroom teacher, and that really is his name. I told his teacher that I wanted to interview him to see if he's related to the real Walt Disney, how having that name has affected his life, and what he thinks about the impact that vision and imagination can have on the world. His teacher was really nice and said she'd talk to Walt. I gave her my phone number and email, so hopefully I'll be able to talk to Walt soon. Wait a minute, I might meet Walt Disney. Not the real Walt Disney, but a Walt Disney. I've always wanted to do that. Yep, freaky.

I'm just glad it's lunch now. A little time to chill out with Marli and Leo, and I can just be myself. I feel like I'm looking over my shoulder all day waiting for the next weird thing to happen. Oh crap, speaking of weird…here comes Alex.

"Tayleigh, can I talk to you a minute?" asked Alex as he walked over to our table. "Like over here in private?"

"I wonder what that's all about," said Marli. "Don't take too long, we have to head to math soon."

I walked over near Alex and leaned against the wall. "Are you going to admit to me that Vanessa put you up to teasing me about my jeans?" I asked him.

"Just the opposite," said Alex. "I seriously do want to get those jeans for my sister's birthday. You have such great style, so I know she'll like them. To prove to you that I'm being straight with you, I brought you something." He handed me a piece of paper all folded up. I started getting a little panicky thinking he may have written some weird love note or something.

"What is it? Just tell me," I demanded.

"You're going to have a pop quiz next hour in math. Those are all of the answers to the quiz. I'm helping you out so you'll help me out," Alex replied.

"You gotta be kidding me!" I almost shouted but then realized I should talk a little more quietly. "I don't cheat. I don't want these answers."

"You do with them what you want, but they're yours now. Just please tell me about the jeans!" Alex begged.

"Whatever. Aeropostale," I answered.

"Cool. Thanks. Good luck on your quiz," Alex offered as he walked away. I quickly shoved the folded piece of paper in my pocket as I walked back to the table and grabbed my laptop and books.

"Let's get moving to class," I said to Marli. "We'll see you later, Leo."

"What was that all about?" asked Leo.

"Nothing. He's just weird. Catch you later," I said and gave Leo one last kiss before heading off to math.

"Really, what was it about?" asked Marli in a hushed voice as we walked away. "He doesn't like you, does he? If he does, it's totally not fair! You already have a boyfriend, and I think Alex is cute. Why does everyone have to like you?"

"Oh hush up, Marli. It's not that at all. Alex insisted he really does like my jeans, and to prove it he gave me the answers to our math quiz," I whispered. "I told him I don't cheat, but he wouldn't take the answers back. It was all just very bizarre."

"Oh good. I mean, not so good. Hey, I'll take the answers," joked Marli. "Actually, I think I'm ready for any quiz after your Aunt Leigh's help the other night."

I like math okay. Well, some math. I liked algebra a lot because I totally understood equations and that kind of stuff. I just get really nervous when it's quiz or test time. I feel like I understand it all when I'm at Aunt Leigh's house, then test time comes and I just lose all confidence. That's what I'm doing now…losing confidence. I'm looking at this pop quiz, and I swear it's all in a foreign language. Breathe. Just breathe.

I have to remind myself of that so I don't hyperventilate, which has happened before and it's not a pretty sight. Marli is writing a lot over there. She must understand it. Why can't I remember how to do this?

I wish I didn't freak out on tests. I need to stand up and stretch or something. Maybe that'll help.

"Tayleigh, where do you think you're going?" questioned Mrs. Shelby.

"I'm not going anywhere. I just can't think, and I thought it might help if I stretched," I explained.

"Please sit back down and finish your quiz," she ordered. She's a nice teacher, and she really does help me a lot in math. I know she can't play favorites or anything. Fine, I'll sit back down, but I don't think it's going to help anything.

"Tayleigh is cheating!" shouted Vanessa, who sits right behind me in math.

"I am not!" I shouted back. "I was just stretching. I didn't look at anyone's paper or anything."

"Mrs. Shelby," tattled Vanessa, "I just saw that paper fall out of Tayleigh's pocket, and I can see it has math on it!"

Mrs. Shelby walked over and picked up the folded piece of paper near my desk. She opened it, and I could see the shock on her face.

"It's not mine. Honestly, I didn't cheat," I tried to explain.

"Tayleigh, you may take your books down to the office and sit there until I come down to sort this all out," ordered Mrs. Shelby.

Tears immediately fill my eyes. I've never been sent to the principal's office for doing something wrong. I'd never cheat. Everyone in the class is staring at me, except Marli. Marli can't even look at me because she knows the truth, and I know she doesn't want to get in trouble too. I can't believe this is happening to me. I will not cry out loud. I wish I wasn't here. I wish I wasn't here. I wish I wasn't here. Nope, it's not working. Darn it. I walk down to the principal's office carrying my books and laptop, and I sit down in a chair waiting for Mrs. Shelby.

She came in about ten minutes later. "I have the class working on an assignment now, so we're going to deal with this. Let me go get Mr. Ward so we can all hear this at the same time," she said as she walked towards Mr. Ward's office.

Mr. Ward is the principal. I've talked to him a few times. His daughter is in my grade and in choir with me. He seems nice, but I don't really know him. Right now I'm terrified of him, even though I know I didn't cheat.

"Please come in here, Ms. Vesper," called Mr. Ward from his office. I slowly walked into his office. I know I should walk in proudly with my head held high since I didn't do anything wrong, but I was too nervous to act like that.

Mrs. Shelby pulled out the piece of paper with the quiz answers on it. "This fell out of Tayleigh's pocket when she got up to stretch during our pop quiz today," she explained. "Somehow she has a list of all of the quiz items and their correct answers. Would you like to explain this to us, Tayleigh?" Mrs. Shelby and Mr. Ward turned to look at me, which was pretty intimidating.

"I didn't use the answers," I stammered. Man, I sounded guilty the way I was talking. Toughen up girl. But, I don't want to tell on Alex, either. He's a good guy, and he was trying to be nice to me. "Someone gave that to me right before class. I told that person that I won't cheat, and I just put the paper in my pocket. I didn't even look at it, I promise."

"Who gave you the paper, Tayleigh?" asked Mrs. Shelby. "It's obviously someone from my first block class since that's the only other hour today that had the same quiz."

"I don't want to get anyone in trouble," I mumbled.

"Let me put it to you this way," stated Mr. Ward. "It is your responsibility, as stated in the honor code for the school, not to cheat. It is also your responsibility to report any cheating. While you may not have used the answers that someone gave you, you also didn't turn that paper in to Mrs. Shelby when you got to class. So, you are not innocent in this matter. There will be consequences. The level of your consequences depends on your answer to this question: who gave you the paper?"

Crap oh crap oh crap! I'm in trouble anyway. Just because I didn't turn in the paper? Here come those tears again. I can't believe I'm going to get into trouble. I don't want it to be worse. I'm sorry Alex, but I have to tell. "Alex Walker gave it to me before class," I said quietly. I didn't want to be a tattletale, but I didn't want to get in even more trouble when I didn't cheat.

"Good choice, Ms. Vesper. You may go wait in a chair outside my office while Mrs. Shelby and I discuss the consequences for your actions," said Mr. Ward.

Punishment! I sat down in one of the chairs outside of the principal's office and tried not to cry too loudly. I usually like to tell my parents about my day at school, but now I have no desire to talk to them at all. They're going to be so disappointed in me. Mr. Ward is right. I should have turned in the paper when I first got to math class. I just wasn't thinking. I wasn't planning to look at it. I was just going to throw it out. Why didn't I throw it out? I wish I could go back and have a redo. I either wouldn't have taken it in the first place or I would have ripped it up and thrown it out right away.

Mrs. Shelby opened the door and called me back in. "I believe you when you say you didn't cheat," said Mrs. Shelby, "but that's not how it looked. You made the right choice by telling us who gave you the answers, but you should have given me the paper when you first got to class."

"In the student handbook, cheating means a five day suspension," said Mr. Ward. My tears started flowing even faster. "However, since you did not actually cheat, I am not going to enforce that statute. However, as a reminder that you have the responsibility to live up to the honor code, you are suspended from the dance team for the rest of the season."

That's it, I started bawling out loud. I love dance. I'm good at dance. The dance team needs me.

"Calm down, Ms. Vesper," said Mr. Ward. "The suspension from the dance team does not go on your permanent record. A suspension from school would be on your permanent record, which could affect college admissions and scholarships. Do you understand? I have taken into consideration that you are typically a good student, and I didn't want this to negatively impact your future. However, you need to learn your lesson. You may sit in the office the rest of this class period to collect yourself, then you can go on to your fifth block."

"Tayleigh, you're also going to get an E on this quiz. I hope you understand what you did was wrong, but I'm proud that you made the right choice in the end," said Mrs. Shelby as she put her arms around my shoulders for a little hug. "I'll see you tomorrow in class."

"Thank you, Mr. Ward. Thank you, Mrs. Shelby," I quietly said in between sobs and sniffles as I walked back outside of Mr. Ward's office.

I just sat and stared at the wall for the rest of fourth block, however long that was. I feel so…lost. I just can't believe this happened to me.

I stopped at my locker on the way to gym to grab my gym bag. I felt like I was moving in slow motion, but at least my body knew what I needed to get even if my brain wasn't connecting right now.

"Omigosh, Tay," cried Marli. "What happened? How are you doing?" She threw her arms around me and looked like she was going to cry, too. "Vanessa is probably behind all of this. I bet she told Alex to give you the answers just so you'd get in trouble. Then she pulled them out of your pocket or something. She's always out to get you!"

"I'm suspended from dance for the rest of the season," I said slowly.

"The season just began. That means you're not going to dance at any basketball games?" asked Marli.

"I had to turn in Alex, too, otherwise it would have been worse for me. At least they believed me that I didn't cheat," I said.

"Harsh. Suspended from dance for not cheating. What's up with that?" pondered Marli. I went ahead and gave her the quick run down of what happened as we headed to gym. My mind was wandering and I was hoping we had to run laps today in gym. I could use the mindless exercise.

"I guess it's better than being suspended from school, but it still sucks," agreed Marli. "I wonder what's going to happen to Alex. I bet he gets suspended from school. Unless it really was all Vanessa's fault…wouldn't it be great to see her get in trouble? Maybe we can help prove that this was all Vanessa's idea."

"At this point, I don't care, and I don't want to know any more about it," I said as I changed into my gym uniform.

"I love your uniform today. You just wear it with such style, Tayleigh. You just look so cute," said Brittany as she walked by my gym locker.

"Oh shut up," I snapped. "Sorry, Brit, I didn't mean that. It's just been a rough afternoon."

"Well, it really does look cute," Brittany said in a much smaller voice, and then she turned and walked away quickly.

I walked into the gym and just started running. I didn't even hear what we were supposed to be doing, but since running laps is punishment for not paying attention – I figure I can't go wrong with running laps. Just so much to think about. How am I going to tell my parents about this? How are my friends on the dance team going to take this? If one of us is gone, it throws off the whole dance. They're going to have to relearn everything without me. It was just so stupid of me. I never was going to cheat anyway, but I shouldn't have put that paper from Alex in my pocket. I was inviting disaster to happen.

"TAYLEIGH!" hollered Marli as she grabbed the back of my shirt. "Go shower! You've been running for 50 minutes straight. You have to be exhausted."

"Class is over already?" I asked. "I feel like I just started running. I've been thinking about everything that happened today. I don't know what I'm going to do when I get home. My parents are going to be so disappointed."

"They'll still love you," said Marli. "You'll probably be grounded, too. Although, maybe they'll realize that being kicked off the dance team is punishment enough."

"Do you really think Vanessa put Alex up to bugging me and giving me the answers?" I asked. "She can seem mean at times, but I don't think she's honestly a mean or conniving person. I think she's just a snob."

"I'll do some fact checking. You know I'm great at figuring out what's going on. Okay, maybe I'm not the one who is so great at it, but I know who is. I'll go talk to Brittany. She's in my next hour, and she always knows everything," suggested Marli.

"Thanks, you're a good friend," I said. "I wish that science will go by slowly. I don't really want to go home today." I turned to wave Marli off as I stopped at my locker. I was putting in my combination when Leo walked up. He gave me a big hug.

"Is it true? It just doesn't sound like you, so I won't believe anything until I hear it from you. Did you cheat? Are you off the dance team?" asked Leo, holding my chin in his hand.

"I didn't cheat. I did have the answers, but I didn't use them. And yes, I am kicked off the dance team for not turning in the answers and telling who gave them to me up front," I answered.

"I knew you didn't cheat," Leo said. "There's no way. Isn't that a pretty big punishment for not cheating? You didn't want to be a tattletale, I'm sure."

"That's what I thought, but Principal Ward said it's part of the honor code. He said he could have suspended me from school for not turning in Alex when he first gave me the answers. So, I guess I was lucky," I replied.

"Do you want some good news before you head off to science? It might make the rest of the day go better. Or, I can wait until after school to tell you," offered Leo.

"I could use some good news. I'm not sure I'll process it all as my brain keeps thinking about how I'm going to tell my parents about all of this," I said.

Leo nodded knowingly. He understood how hard it was going to be for me to disappoint my parents. "This might make it easier," he offered. "I also heard another rumor that you might become an honorary band member. It seems that your singing is so good, your choir teacher talked to my band director about having you sing a few solos accompanied by the band at our next concert. We've never done this before, so it could be pretty cool. Plus, it would mean I'd see you more often at band practices!"

"Great, something else for me to be nervous about. I'm already nervous enough about singing one little solo at the choir concert. Plus, I don't know if the principal will let me do anything special like that now," I said.

"Ah, good point. I hear this rumor earlier today – before I heard about your bad news. Well, I still hope it works out," encouraged Leo.

“I better get to science. I’ll see you after school. Do you have practice today?” I asked.

“Yes, we do. But, there’s enough time for me to drop you off at your house first, if you want,” said Leo.

“Thanks, I appreciate it. Obviously I don’t have to stay after school for dance practice now. Since I’m in no hurry to get home today, I think I’ll just take the bus. I’ll give you a call later, though, unless all of my phone privileges are taken away,” I muttered.

I think the whole school knows about what happened in math class. I haven’t seen Alex at all, so I’m assuming he’s either in Mr. Ward’s office or his parents already came to get him. He’s normally in my science class, so something must have happened to him.

What a boring lecture today. I guess I got my wish. Science is dragging by. I don’t even know what the lecture is on…something to do with volcanoes or volcanic layers or something like that. I guess I’ll have to read it later in my science book. I like science. In fact I like it enough that I’m in an advanced class, but I just can’t focus right now. Great, that means I’ll have to take my science book home too. Having this laptop is great, but carrying it everywhere means stuff is getting a little too heavy. I should have taken Leo up on the ride home. Since I’m sure I’ll be grounded anyway, I’ll probably get the laptop taken away and be stuck in my room. Great, I’ll have science to read. Yippee. And everyone else can enjoy the no homework rule right now, but because I’m zoning out in class – I get to do some homework. I should stop having this conversation with myself and listen. Maybe I can catch up. Nope, I think I'm too far lost. What a waste of a day.

"Ouch," I said quietly. Jessica, who sits next to me just hit my arm. It didn't really hurt, but it startled me.

"This is from Morgan," Jessica whispered as she handed me a folded note.

The note said:

I heard what happened in math. It's so not fair! You didn't even cheat. As team captain, I can tell you that you're still a dance team member, even if you can't perform. I'll still invite you to our parties. It's going to be such a mess to try to change the choreography to fill your place. You're so going to be missed, Tay! We love you! Morgan

I looked over at Morgan and gave her a half smile. She's really nice. Almost everyone on the team is great, and I've danced with some of them at the studio since I was three years old. I knew they'd be on my side, but it was nice to know it for sure. I wanted to write her a note back and tell her thanks, but with my luck today – I'd probably get caught for that and in even more trouble. I definitely don't need that. I'm sure she understands. It was really nice of her to tell me the team is still with me.

When the bell rang, Morgan walked over to me and gave me a big hug. “You’ll make it through this,” she said. She sounded so mature. She is a senior, so I guess she should be.

“I needed that. Thanks,” I said. “I don’t have time to chat today. I have to catch the bus home now. Obviously I’m not staying for practice.”

“I’d offer you a ride, but I do have to get to practice. Wouldn’t look good for the captain to show up late. Plus, we have so much work to do now without you there. Sorry. Didn’t mean to make you feel worse,” Morgan said sheepishly.

“I get it. Go. Get to work. I’ll cheer you guys on from the stands at the next game,” I half shouted as I walked away from her. I tried to act like I didn’t care, but it was tearing me up inside.

Marli was at the lockers when I got there getting her stuff ready to take to band. “Where’s Leo? Isn’t he taking you home before band practice?” inquired Marli.

“No, I said I’d ride the bus. I’m not in any hurry to get home, so I figured the bus ride would take longer,” I replied.

“Want me to come over and be with you when you tell your parents?” asked Marli. Is she a great friend, or what?

“I’m sure Mr. Ward has already called them, so they probably know his version of the story. You were there. You know what happened. I guess it couldn’t hurt to have you be with me too, if you really don’t mind," I responded. "I'd appreciate it. Oh wait, you have band practice. You can't skip that, then you'll get in trouble too."

"I'm always there for you, sis," Marli said as she hip bumped me. Then she grabbed my scarf and started pulling me to the bus. "Let's get moving. Don't worry about band. I'll text Mr. Shets that I have a sore throat and need to go home. We still have a few weeks until the concert, so these are totally critical practices yet. My girl needs me more!"

I weakly smiled at Marli. I sure do love that girl. I hope she knows how much I appreciate her. I just don't have the energy to show her right now.

I always dread the bus ride home, which is why I love it when I have dance practice or get a ride from Leo or Bryant. The bus stinks, everyone is noisy, and I'm one of the last stops. I swear the night just zipped by. Marli and I were talking a bit, but I think I mostly just spaced out because before I knew it – we were at our stop.

Marli put her arm around me as we walked to my front door. "Your parents are so cool, it'll be fine," she said as she opened the door. "Hello, Mrs. Vesper!"

My mom was walking towards the front hall, she obviously heard us open the door. "Hi, Marli. I don't mean to be rude, but you can't stay today. I need to talk to Tayleigh," Mom directed as she held the door open for Marli to leave.

"I'm here for you in spirit," Marli whispered to me and left. Now I felt extra bad. Marli skipped band practice to be here to support me, and Mom kicked her out right away. Yep, it's a rotten day.

"So, I guess that means you've heard what happened today at school?" I asked.

"Yes, both Mr. Ward and Mrs. Shelby called me today to explain the situation, but I'd like to hear about it from you," said Mom as we walked into the living room. "You know that your father and I love you very much, and we believe in you. I don't want to jump to any conclusions until I've heard from you what happened."

I guess my mom is pretty cool. I know a lot of moms who would have just started yelling and assuming the worst. I explained everything to her, even sharing how bad I felt that I didn't turn in the answer sheet.

"I believe you," she said as she gave me a big hug. "I didn't think you were planning to cheat. That's not the girl we raised. But, I also agree that Mr. Ward had to enforce the no cheating policy since you didn't turn in the answers when you were first given them. It does sound like you understand what you did wrong."

"I do. I do," I said with emphasis. "But it's just not fair that I'm off the dance team. My life is dance!"

"I would say you have more time to spend on homework, but you don't have any homework right now. Well, you can practice your singing for choir," suggested Mom. "Your father and I also spoke this afternoon and we feel that since you're not going to be at dance practice, you should start going back to youth group at church. You used to be so involved in youth group, but we allowed that to slip because of your involvement on the dance team."

"Come on, Mom," I whined. Yes, I whined. "You know the only people who still go to youth group in high school either play in the band with the praise choir or they don't have anything better to do. I'm not in either of those groups. I have other things to do. I can hang out with Marli and Leo. I can watch all of the episode of *Dancing with the Stars* and *American Idol* on the DVR. I can figure out stuff to do."

"We're not punishing you for what happened today. We feel the school appropriately reprimanded you and you've learned your lesson, but we also think going back to youth group will help you focus a little more on the values that are important in life," explained Mom.

"Whatever," I said as I started to sulk off to my room.

"Don't use that tone of voice with me, young lady!" shouted Mom. "You can storm off to your room, but you need to be ready to go in a half hour because there's youth group tonight."

"Can I take Marli or Leo?" I asked. Marli used to go with me when we were little, even though she didn't go to our church. "That way I wouldn't be all alone there."

“You’ll be fine, Tayleigh. Polly and Jason will be there too,” said Mom.

Great, just what I need. Time to hang out with my siblings. Normally I wouldn’t mind that, but I’m just not feeling it right now. Yippee. It makes it even worse to know that a bunch of elementary and middle school kids will be there. I haven’t been in youth group since middle school, but now that I’m in high school – I don’t want to hang around with the younger kids. I guess I shouldn’t complain too much. Mom did understand and believe me. Obviously she and Dad already figured out the truth since they’d talked about not punishing me. But youth group – ugh!

Mom, Jason, Polly, and I walked out to the garage to get into the car. Polly and Jason quietly got into the back seat.

“What’s going on?” I wondered. “Usually one of you is calling shotgun and pushes everyone else out of the way to sit in the front.”

“It’s been like this for a few days,” Mom said. “I’ve always wanted them to get along a little more, but it’s almost like they don’t care. I’m going to talk to their teachers tomorrow at school to see if anything is going on there.”

“There’s nothing, Mom. I just don’t need to be first or in front or win,” said Polly.

“Ya, Mom. We’ve realized that it doesn’t really matter,” said Jason.

"It's just not normal," I said. "This is taking it all to the extreme."

"It just must be your lucky week, less fighting for you to referee," said Polly. "It's my lucky week, too. I'm so glad you're coming to youth group. It's been so long since you've come to youth group, and I've missed you. I always do everything with Jason, so it'll be fun to do something with you now. Too bad Bryant isn't here, too."

"I didn't think of it that way," I replied. "You're right, we can have some fun. I'll try, at least."

"Tonight we're voting on our executive committee," offered Jason. "Polly and I were both going to give speeches tonight to try to convince everyone to elect one of us as president, but I don't think I want to do that any more. Plus, we're some of the youngest kids there, so we probably didn't have a real chance anyway."

"Yep," concurred Polly. "Hey, you should be president, Tay! You'd be great! You're probably going to be one of the oldest kids there, so everyone will listen to you."

"No, definitely not. No interest in that here," I confessed. Are they crazy? I didn't even want to come to youth group, let alone be the youth group president.

"Even if you're not interested in the executive committee, Tayleigh, I hope you'll try hard to be involved and participate. I don't want to hear you were sulking in the corner or anything like that," said Mom. "You used to love youth group. Just try to have a good time."

"I think it's going to be great!" exclaimed Polly.

"Me too," added Jason. "We never get to see you anymore so it'll be fun."

They're right. High school definitely has changed me that way. Marli and I used to hang out with Polly and Jason all of the time. Marli would even joke that Jason was her real best friend. We're so busy with stuff in high school now that we rarely do anything with the twins. It's not that I don't like them, I actually really like hanging out with them…for the most part. I guess I'll try to be positive for them. It's so much better than the awful punishment I kept imagining all the way home. I'd still rather be at dance, but there's nothing I can do about that.

"We'll have a good time," I said as I turned around and smiled at the twins in the backseat.

"I nominate Tayleigh for president," said Jason. "She's been in youth group since she was in elementary school, so she knows everything about it. She's in high school, so that means she knows a lot too."

"She's also got extra time on her hands since there's no homework at the high school right now," added Polly.

"Wait a minute," I interjected. "I didn't even say I was interested in being president. This is my first youth group meeting in more than six months. I'm sure a lot of things have changed. I don't want to come in here and think I could be president now." Yep, I think that sounded pretty mature. I didn't tell them I thought youth group was for losers, I made them think I wasn't good enough to be president. Looking around the room, though, it was a bunch of little kids, a few high school losers, and me. I thought the praise band kids would at least be here, but it turns out that they have band practice at the same time. So, there are a few kids here who aren't involved in anything at school so they come to youth group. I can't believe I have to hang out with all of them now. That doesn't mean I'll start hanging out with them at school. Wow, that sounded snobby. I'm not a snob. Now I'm going to have to force myself to say hi to them at school just to prove to myself that I'm not a snob. We're just not all going to be new best friends because of youth group.

"We all know how involved you've been in youth group in past years," said Garrett, our youth group leader. "If you want to run for president, I think that's completely fine. It sounds like your siblings are great campaign managers."

"Please, please, please, Tay!" whined Polly.

"Okay, put my name on the list," I conceded. There's no way I'll be picked. I haven't been here in so long, and there are other kids who really want to be president.

"Let me add Tayleigh's name on the board here," said Garrett. "I think that completes our slate of nominations. I need everyone to get a piece of paper here to write your choices on. Remember, the person who gets the most votes will be our president, second most will be vice president, and third most will be treasurer."

Since there are five people on the list, there's a good chance I'll be one of the two who don't get picked for anything. I know everyone here. I've been going to church with them forever. They have to realize that I don't want to be president. I just rejoined youth group tonight, so I definitely wouldn't be the right person to pick.

Voting went really fast. All 26 kids put their ballots in the box, and Garrett started reading them out loud. It reminded me of the ceremony on the TV show, *Survivor*. Here I am hoping I'll be voted off the island! I wonder what Marli and Leo are doing right now. Leo should be done with band practice. Marli is probably chasing her cats around the house since she skipped band. I wish they could have come to youth group. I'll invite them to come next time. Mom can't be mad at me for that. You don't turn people away from church, so if they want to be here – they can be here. Maybe that's a little sneaky, but I think it'll work.

"It looks like we have our president," announced Garrett. "Welcome back, Tayleigh, and congratulations!" Jason leaned over and gave me a high five while Polly threw her arms around me for a big hug. Crap. Why does this have to happen to me?

"Um…thanks," I muttered. I wasn't sure what to say. "I guess I need to find out exactly what the president does since I wasn't planning on this."

"We can work as a team," said Amber. She got the vice president position. "And since you brought your computer with you, we can start typing out some ideas right now." Yes, I brought my Mac with me. I'm not sure why. I just didn't feel right leaving it at home alone.

"Sounds good to me. Thanks," I replied.

"Can you believe they elected me president?" I asked Marli on the phone. I texted her from youth group, but sometimes you just gotta talk on the phone, so I called her as soon as I got home.

"Just the other day I was wishing I could be President…of the United States, that is," Marli laughed.

"I don't think youth group comes close to that. Maybe I can do it for a little while and then slowly fade away so Amber can take over," I suggested. "She really wanted to be president. She's in 8th grade, so it's not like she's super busy yet."

"That's a great idea," said Marli. "But, who knows, once I come back to youth group, maybe we can make it fun."

"You're really going to come?" I asked. "Thank you so much! You're the best!"

"Yep, I know. I always liked your youth group, so why not. Plus, with you in charge, we can plan some fun things and maybe get some other people to come," said Marli.

"I didn't think of it that way," I replied. "You and Polly are really helping me look at things with the glass half full tonight. I didn't want to go to youth group at all, but Polly said I haven't been hanging around with her enough lately so she was really excited for me to go. I guess I have been pretty wrapped up in my own world. But, back to my own world, if Leo comes too, it'll be perfect. Time with the twins, my best friend, and my boyfriend…sounds good to me!"

"Speaking of Leo, do you want to go shopping tomorrow night for Winter Carnival? We need our dresses otherwise I'm going to end up wearing jeans!" exclaimed Marli.

"Most definitely!" I squealed. "Just a minute…Mom, can Marli and I go shopping tomorrow night? We need to get our Winter Carnival dresses…She said yes! She said Bryant can drop us off at the mall if we need a ride."

"Perfect. I like Leo, but I didn't really want him going with us," said Marli.

"No way. Dress shopping is totally a girl thing," I agreed. "I don't really want our moms there either. You know they make us try on dresses they think are cute but aren't really. I guess I'm pretty lucky. I thought I was going to be grounded, and here I am planning a shopping trip with you!"

"Your parents rock!" exclaimed Marli. "Alright, madam president, I'll see you in the morning. Is Leo picking you up? Can I grab a ride?"

"Yep. Be here at 7:10am. See ya," I said as I hung up.

CHAPTER 5

"Are you coming to band practice after school today?" asked Leo as we drove to school.

"I totally forgot about that and made other plans," I complained. Who has band practice on a Friday anyway? Aren't Fridays supposed to be all about fun? I guess no one told their band director that.

"With me!" interrupted Marli. "Oh wait, I guess I have band too then. Oops, I forgot too. I skip it one day then totally space and forget I still have practice. I guess I can't claim to be sick two days in a row."

"We were planning to go to the mall to pick out dresses for the dance after school. Bryant was going to drop us off," I explained to Leo. "With everyone else that has been going on, I forgot that Ms. Planter called last night and explained about me singing with the band."

"This is one of only two after school practices for the concert," said Leo. "You have to be there if you're going to sing with us. You said you always wanted to be in band. This is your chance. I know it's not critical. I mean, it'll be awesome to have you sing, but we'll still play the same song even if no one sings with it. It would just make it better with you singing."

"We can go shopping afterwards," suggested Marli. "Remember, no homework means for extra long evenings!"

"Great point, Mar! Practice is done by 4:30pm, isn't it?" I asked Leo.

"I'd be happy to drop you guys off at the mall after practice. I won't invade your space. You can either call Bryant or me when you're done," smiled Leo. Isn't he in tune with what I want? I didn't even tell him that I don't want him to go shopping with us. He just knew.

"That works for me," said Marli. "I'll text my mom to tell her what we'll be up to – you know how she worries sometimes."

"I'll text my folks, too. Hopefully they'll see me as being responsible for going to band practice. I'm sure they remembered about it since Mom talked to Ms. Planter last night. They don't need to know that I forgot about it," I reminded Marli and Leo. "Mom was willing to let me go shopping even after the mess yesterday with math class, so I'm sure she'll be okay with us going after band practice."

"Since it's so cold out, I'm going to drop you ladies off at the door. You don't need to be walking through all of this snow," offered Leo.

"Are you the gentleman or what?" smiled Marli. "I knew we kept you around for a reason, now I know what it is."

I leaned over and gave Leo a kiss on his cheek, and he turned quickly so our lips met. He pulled me closer for a longer kiss.

"Not again you guys. I'm going to have to get a separate ride next time," laughed Marli.

"That doesn't count as PDA. It's just you here," I said. "See you later, Leo. Thanks!"

Marli and I headed to Social Studies. We're studying colonial times right now, which is kind of cool. Aunt Leigh and Uncle TJ took me to Virginia one year for vacation, and I got to see the homes of Thomas Jefferson, George Washington, James Madison, and that one President I always forget…another James…I can't remember his name.

"Tayleigh, do you have a minute?" shouted Morgan across the hall. I miss seeing Morgan after school in dance. We don't have any classes together.

"What's up, Morgan? How is dance going?" I asked.

“We definitely miss you already. It’s hard changing the choreography for the dances so there are no holes in our formations. Plus, you’re just fun to be around, so we miss you being there,” replied Morgan.

“I miss you guys, too. Hey, we can all dance together at the school dance,” I offered.

“Sounds good,” smiled Morgan. “I wanted to ask you where you got that skirt, though. It’s so cute. I love how it hugs your body without making you look fat.”

“Are you calling me fat?” I asked, then laughed. “My cousin actually got it for me for my birthday. I’m not sure where she got it.” I was feeling a little dressy today, which is way different from my normal jeans and hoodie. Since Marli and I were planning to go to the mall, I wanted to look good.

“Well, let me know if you find out,” said Morgan. “I’ll see you later.”

Marli is always so quiet when girls from dance are around. I know she doesn’t really know them that well, but I always try to include her in things. I don’t want her to feel left out. “I miss dance, but it does give me more time to hang out with you!” I said as I put my arm around Marli’s shoulder.

“Aren’t you just the fashion queen lately?” joked Marli. “It seems like everyone is asking you where you got your clothes. It’s not like you’re wearing anything different, but suddenly everyone is noticing what you’re wearing.”

"Girls on the dance team are always trading clothes, so I didn't think that was strange. But you're right, between Vanessa and Alex and Ms. Planter and Morgan…hmmm, weird," I agreed. "Let's get to class. I think today we're talking about when Washington, DC was attacked and President Jefferson had to flee to his retreat home. You know I've been to Poplar Forest."

"I know, I know, your awesome trip to Virginia. I wish I could have gone, too. You're so lucky…you have understanding parents and a cool aunt and uncle," dreamed Marli. "You can help me remember this stuff so I'll do well on the next test."

As we walked into Social Studies, Mr. Abrams handed my laptop bag to me. "What?" I asked, quite confused. "Why do you have my computer?"

"Your dad just dropped it off to class," replied Mr. Abrams. "He said you forgot it at home, and he wanted you to have it at school."

"I didn't need it today, though," I said. "Oh well, I guess I'll have to carry it around. It's definitely not something I'm going to leave in my locker." My dad is really thoughtful, but this is the second time he's brought my computer to school when I purposely left it at home. I have to remember to talk to him. It just makes for more stuff that I have to carry, and that's a pain if I don't really need it.

"I thought you said you'd carry your computer everywhere if you got one," teased Marli. "I clearly remember you saying that once upon a time."

"Hey, that means you were actually listening to me sometime," I joked. "I didn't really mean I'd want to take it everywhere. I definitely don't look as good weighed down with a computer bag and my books." That was a big joke because I don't really care that much about how I look. Well, maybe a little. Okay, more than a little. But, a laptop bag doesn't make me look bad, I'm just too lazy to want to carry it everywhere. Yep, that's the real truth.

"Everyone settle down," announced Mr. Abrams. "Now, who remembers the name of the house where President Jefferson fled to? We started talking about it yesterday."

I raised my hand enthusiastically. "Poplar Forest!" I shouted. "I even brought my photo album from my trip there, so we can look at exactly how Mr. Jefferson lived. I know where his horse would have dropped him off and where his French chef worked and even where his indoor privy was…that's a toilet, in case you didn't know." Wow. I totally sounded like a know-it-all. That's not normally me. I couldn't help it. The trip to Virginia was a lot of fun, and I didn't realize how much I actually learned about history when I was there. It was really making this colonial stuff come to life for me.

"Since you're so excited about this, why don't you go ahead and share some of what you learned about President Jefferson and Poplar Forest? You can pass around your photo album as you explain some things," offered Mr. Abrams.

"Thank you. I know I'm usually not that excited about history, but my trip to Virginia made it feel like I know President Jefferson. In fact, I did meet him while I was down there…" I started. I rambled on for almost the whole class period about Jefferson. Wouldn't my aunt and uncle be proud? I'll have to remember to tell them about it later.

At lunch Marli and I were sitting together waiting for Leo to join us. Neither of us was very hungry. These last few days Marli has gotten into the habit of getting us something to eat before school since the cafeteria is open, but then we're not really hungry by lunch time. Thankfully we grab another snack later in the day so we're not starving after school. Aren't mini-meals the way to go anyway? Probably not hot cocoa and candy bars. Ya, we gotta re-evaluate the way we're eating…not the healthiest, that's for sure.

At lunch we like to people watch. We look around at people eating and make up conversations that they're having. The problem is that sometimes we forget we made up the conversation and later we think we heard someone say that. So, we're trying to make up really crazy conversations so we won't get confused with what is real.

"Then I saw Jodi jump off the top of the basketball stands and fly over to the hoop, just sitting there until someone would notice her," said Marli mimicking Samantha's movements as she made up words to go into her mouth.

"Jodi really wanted Nick to notice her as he shot for a basket, but he didn't. She started crying," I said, looking sad like Brooke did. "She cried so much that the basketball floor flooded and the game was cancelled."

We both cracked up. "These stories are getting worse," said Leo as he walked up. "I used to enjoy listening to the two of you, but I think you've lost it." He planted a kiss on my forehead.

"This one was a bit out there, I agree," I said.

"Out there? But it really happened!" argued Marli. "Uh-oh. Don't look now, but here comes Vanessa."

"It's been a good day so far, too. Why'd you have to go ruin it by mentioning her?" I whispered. I refused to turn around, though. Maybe if I didn't look at her, then she really wouldn't be there.

"I didn't do it, Tayleigh. I just wanted you to hear that from me," announced Vanessa.

"Didn't do what?" I asked. Phooey – I responded to her. I didn't mean to. I wasn't even going to acknowledge her, but she made me curious.

"I didn't tell Alex to give you any answers. Even though we're not really friends, I don't cheat and I wouldn't try to get you or Alex in trouble for cheating," Vanessa explained. "I think he really thought he was being nice. Maybe he has a crush on you."

"Not that we'd actually believe anything you'd say," Marli shot back. She's always on my side.

"Whatever. I just wanted to set things straight," said Vanessa as she flipped her hair over her shoulder and stormed off.

Leo looked at both of us and asked, "Did you ever think that she might be telling the truth?"

That broke the tension of the moment. Marli and I cracked up. "Vanessa…tell the truth?" I choked. "I don't think she knows what that is. And, she'd take any opportunity to make me look or feel bad."

"Maybe she's finally realized how poorly she's treated you and is trying to change," Leo suggested. "You said Alex was trying to help you. Maybe he really thought he was in his own misdirected way."

"He's got a point there, Tay, but it's still hard for me to believe Vanessa. I still think she should have been suspended, too. If not for cheating, then for just being a witch," smiled Marli.

"Lunch is almost over. Let's get back to Samantha and Brooke's conversation about Jodi being stuck on top of the basketball hoop with a flooded floor," I said as Leo rolled his eyes. "The half-time buzzer rang and the dance team swam out to do their performance." Marli and I both started laughing again.

Thankfully the rest of the day went by pretty quickly. I have important things to do tonight…like shopping…so I didn't need school to get in the way! First I had to go to band rehearsal. I'm pretty nervous about this. I only discovered a few days ago that I do have a good voice, so my confidence level isn't too high yet. At least Marli is going to be there too – it's always good to bring your own cheering section.

"Can't I just stand next to you in the trumpet section? I'd feel much safer," I suggested.

"I doubt it. Unfortunately, you'll probably be standing right next to Mr. Shets, which means you'll be in the front of the room," explained Marli. "Not trying to make you more nervous – I'm just trying to prepare you."

"Why did I say yes? If I was still on the dance team, then I couldn't do this and life would be so much better," I whined. Yes, I whined again. What's up with my whininess?

"My little Suzy Snowflake will be wonderful," gushed Leo as he walked out from the band room and took my hand. "Let me introduce you to Mr. Shets. I think we're working on the song you're doing first."

"I don't even know what song I'm doing yet," I complained. "I haven't practiced anything. Omigosh! I'm going to look and sound like a total fool." I buried my head in Leo's shoulder.

He grabbed me by the shoulders, turned me to him, and said, "You're good. You wouldn't have been invited here if you weren't good. Marli and I are here for you. Just think about us. Don't think about anyone else. We know you can do it." Marli moved in then and we had a little group hug. I love my little group.

"You must be Tayleigh," said Mr. Shets as he walked over to us. "I've heard great things about you from Ms. Planter. I'm going to give you a few minutes to look over the song I've picked out for the band to do with you. I'll run through the song with the band, then we'll have you join us. So, just take a seat over there, relax, and listen to the music."

That definitely made me feel better. I guess Mr. Shets understood how nervous I was. At least I can listen for a little bit first. I looked down at the sheet of music as Marli and Leo went to their sections, and I saw that the song was Little Drummer Boy. That's the other one of my favorite Christmas songs, and I have my very own little drummer boy in the band! Maybe this was going to be okay. The song didn't have any high notes, either, so I think I can do this.

I kind of zoned out a bit while the band went through the song. I was singing it in my head and not really paying attention to anything Mr. Shets was saying to the band…until I realized he was talked to me. "I'm sorry, Mr. Shets, I was singing the song in my head. Could you please repeat what you just said?"

"I asked if you're ready to try it with us, but it sounds like you are," Mr. Shets said smiling. "Why don't you come over here and stand by Leo?"

I hadn't noticed that Leo moved his snare drum to the front of the band by Mr. Shets. Normally percussion is in the back. I gave a confused look to Leo and Mr. Shets.

"He moved me to the front to be the little drummer boy since there are a few snare solos in the song as well. We'll get to stand next to each other for the song," Leo explained. I just smiled and looked back at Marli, then I smiled even bigger when she winked at me.

The band ran through the song a few times, and I felt really good about my singing. It's like this was all made just for me. My favorite Christmas song, standing next to my man, in the band with my best friend...perfect.

After band practice I grabbed Leo's hand on one side and Marli's hand on the other side and literally felt like skipping to the car. "With the way today has gone, I just know we're going to find the perfect dresses, Marli!" I sang. Yes, I sang it. Not sure if it was a real tune, but I was in the moment.

"She's all yours, Marli," laughed Leo. "She's a little too silly for me right now." But, even as he was teasing me, he gave me a hug and quick kiss before opening my door. I grabbed him and dipped him down for another kiss. Yep, I was definitely in a silly mood.

"Come on!" shouted Marli. "The dresses are calling to me." Marli closed the car door and we started off to the mall.

"Are you going to spend your money on a dress when you don't have a date yet?" asked Leo. "I'm sure you'll have a date, but the dance is only a week away."

I looked angrily at Leo and said, "Of course Marli will have a date. Some wonderful guy just hasn't worked up the nerve to ask her yet!"

"I was kind of hoping that Alex would ask me, but now he's suspended from school. Maybe I should text him and just chat, then it could casually come up in conversation. I could tell him that you're sorry he got caught," suggested Marli.

"I don't know if I want you getting in the middle of that. I should talk to him myself, but I was just going to wait until he came back to school," I said.

"Either way, I'm buying a dress. And, if I don't have a date, I'll go by myself and still have a wonderful time," stated Marli. She has such confidence, it's amazing.

"If you don't have a date, then I guess I'll be the luckiest guy there and have two dates," smiled Leo. Wow, did he just say that? Is he perfect, or what? I'm so glad that he and Marli get along. It would be pure misery if my best friend and boyfriend hated each other. I wish everything in my life was going this well.

"I have to say, though," continued Leo, "I'm so glad I'm not going with you two to the mall. Too much girlie stuff for me right now. Call me when you're ready to leave, and I'll come get you."

"Don't worry about it," I said. "I think we'll call one of our moms to come get us. It's nice to get their opinion of our dresses before we buy them. We'll try on a bunch then call them to come see the ones we really want."

"Always good to involve the moms…especially when they're paying the bill," laughed Marli.

"See you later, Leo. Thanks for the ride," I said as I kissed him one more time. "You have to wait to see the dress until next week!" I did a Vanessa-style toss of my air and sashayed away with Marli into the mall.

Before we even got to the first store, Amber tapped me on the shoulder. "I'm just so excited that we're going to be serving together on the youth group board." She turned to Marli then. "You heard that Tayleigh is president and I'm vice president, right?" Amber always has tried to be close friends with me, but Marli has always been my best friend. Amber is a year younger and she's fun to hang around, but she's no Marli.

"Yep, Tay told me. I think I'm going to start coming back to youth group, too. It'll be fun," Marli replied.

Amber looked a little bummed out. She probably thought we'd bond in youth group. "It'll be fun with all of us. With you and I at the helm and Marli there to support us, we'll make it a good time. I know Polly can't wait for us to plan something fantastic," I offered.

Marli changed the subject, "So what are you doing at the mall, Amber? We're looking for dresses for the dance next week."

"No dance in middle school. I can't wait until next year when I'm at the high school. Maybe we can look for dresses together then," Amber dreamed. "I'm just waiting for a couple of friends. We're going to see the new X-Men movie."

"Awesome!" I replied. "Wolverine is hot! I've been wanting to see that movie."

"We could come back to the mall tomorrow. After all, it's Saturday, and I don't have any plans," suggested Marli.

"Leo and I were going to go bowling tomorrow night – you know, the glo-bowling under the black lights. But, other than that, I don't have any plans either. Let's do it! Do you mind if we go to the movie with you and your friends?" I asked Amber.

"Mind? Do I mind? Are you crazy?" Amber shrieked. "This is great! There's Dana, Katy, and Hannah over there. They won't mind either. Let's go."

So much for dress shopping. Sometimes you gotta make a change for a hot man in a superhero costume. Priorities. It's all about priorities.

Amber's mom gave us a ride home after the movies, which worked out just fine. Marli went home since it was getting pretty late, and I was starting to feel a little bummed that we didn't look for dresses. What if all of the good dresses were taken? I kind of wish we had looked for dresses, but Wolverine sure did look good.

"Do you want to go to the mall with us tomorrow to help us look for dresses, Mom?" I asked. Some teens wouldn't want to be caught in a mall with their mothers, but mine was okay. Plus, she'd already agreed to pay for the dress, so I figure some quality time with her might encourage her to pay for some new shoes too. And, I just like my mom. I really do.

"Jason has a hockey tournament tomorrow out of town. Your father and I are going to that. Polly is going over to stay at Allie's house for the day. Bryant is getting together with a few of the other high school students going to U of M early – it's nice that there's three of them locally so they can do some planning together. You're on your own, kiddo," responded Mom. "I'll give you some money so you can buy the dress or you can put it on hold and we'll go back and get it on Sunday. By the way, I should fill you in on something that happened with the twins today."

"What's going on?" I asked.

"I took them to school this morning so I could talk to their teacher, and he suggested moving them to a private school next year so they can get more personalized attention. He said they're really talented, which of course we knew. But recently since they haven't been fighting as much, he's noticed just how talented they are. He thinks the middle school won't challenge them enough, so he wants us to start thinking about it now," explained Mom.

"Wow," I sighed. I said wow but I was thinking that life isn't fair. Bryant is going to college early because he's so smart, and now the twins are so smart. I'm just Ms. Mediocre. Wait, I guess I'm not. I'm singing solos in choir and band. I'm talented, too. Okay, I can be happy for them. "I'm just part of one smart family. If they do go to the other school, at least they won't have to go to that awful middle school."

"We know you did," commented Mom. "That's one of the reasons your father and I are going to seriously consider the idea of sending the twins elsewhere."

"Not to change the subject…but can we change the subject back to me?" I asked. "Can I call Aunt Leigh to see if she wants to go to the mall with us tomorrow?"

"It's pretty last minute, but go ahead and try. It's not too late to call over there," Mom replied. "Make sure she understands that she doesn't have to pay for anything, though. I don't want her to think you're just inviting her for her credit card!"

"Mom!" I yelled acting all appalled. "Like I would do that. Geesh. Give me a little credit." Okay, I would do that. Aunt Leigh and Uncle TJ do buy us a lot of stuff, but Mom already said she was buying this dress – I wasn't going to double dip. I'm not that greedy.

I grabbed the phone and ran off to my room to call Aunt Leigh.

"So, are you free then? It could be fun. You could try on some clothes too," I suggested.

"I don't think the mall in Battle Creek has enough dress options for your first high school dance. What do you think about taking the train into Chicago for the day and doing some serious shopping on Michigan Avenue?" asked Aunt Leigh.

"Are you serious? OMIGOSH! If Mom says yes, then I'm in. I'm sure Marli's mom will be cool with it too," I yelled as I ran downstairs to ask Mom.

"Your uncle and I were already going to Chicago for the day just to wander around downtown and eat some good food. It would be fun to have you girls tag along," said Aunt Leigh. "The train leaves really early, though, around 7am. Can you get up that early on a Saturday?"

"To go to Chicago? Yes!" I squealed. I explained the situation to Mom, and she said it was fine. I immediately called Marli to ask her, and her mom said it was okay too. Wow, what a change in weekend plans. This is awesome! I better get to bed now if I want to be awake with the appropriate make-up on, a hairstyle that will go with any dress I try on, and an outfit that's ready to take Michigan Avenue by storm!

CHAPTER 6

I'm going to Chicago. I'm going to Chicago. I need a song to sing. What's a Chicago song? Oh ya…*hey hey, holy mackerel, no doubt about it, the Cubs are on their way…* Okay, that's about the only Chicago song I know. And the only reason I know it is because my whole family loves the Chicago Cubs. Usually when we go to Chicago, it's to go to a Cubs game. But not this time. This time is about shopping! YEAH!!!

"Marli is here," yelled Mom. "I don't think I've ever seen her awake at this hour of the day." Aunt Leigh said they'd be by to pick us up at 6:40am so we could get to the train station in time. "Come to think of it," shouted my Mom up the stairs, "I can't remember the last time you've been up and ready to go this early either!"

"Ha ha, Mom. Tell Jason good luck at hockey when he wakes up. I'm tempted to go dump a cold glass of water on him to wish him luck myself, but then he'd be cranky and might not play so well. So tell him that, too. I thought of him," I said as I bopped down the stairs. "Good morning, Marli! Beautiful day, isn't it?"

"It will be, I'm sure," drowsily said Marli. "I just need to wake up a little more. We can sleep on the train, right?"

"Leigh and TJ just pulled up. Get out there, girls, so they don't have to waste time coming in," pushed Mom. She walked out the door with us and gave her sister a hug, "Thanks again for taking the girls."

"We were going anyway with no real agenda. It'll be fun," smiled Aunt Leigh. "Will you give this little good luck package to Jason? Also tell Bryant that we want to hear all about this U of M deal. He hasn't been over yet to tell us what's going on. TJ wants to know what dorm he'll be staying in – of course he's curious if it'll be his old dorm."

"Why won't you both come over for lunch tomorrow after church, then Jason can tell you all about his game and Bryant can explain about U of M. I don't think Polly will be back from Allie's yet. They're going to Allie's parents' cabin for the weekend," suggested Mom.

"Can we just stay the night at Aunt Leigh's house, then, Mom?" I asked.

"No, I want you to come home tonight," Mom replied.

"But…" I whined.

"No buts. You have a youth group meeting before church tomorrow, and I don't want you to miss that, Madam President," ordered Mom.

"Oh ya, I forgot. Oops, I also forgot to let Leo know we're going out of town today. What time will we be back?" I asked.

"That depends if we catch the 6pm or 8pm train, but we definitely won't be home before 10pm," responded Aunt Leigh.

"No glo-bowl for you," said Marli. "It starts at 9pm."

"If we get back at 10pm, maybe I could still go for a little while. What do you think, Mom?" I pleaded.

"Curfew is 11pm, you know that…unless you're still riding home on the train, we'll make an exception for that. But if you're home and out with Leo, then curfew is 11pm," reminded Mom.

"Okay, I'll just text him and tell him to forget it. We can glo-bowl anytime. A trip to Chi-town doesn't come around every week!" I exclaimed.

"Enough talking, let's get moving girls," yelled Uncle TJ from the car. "We have 10 minutes or we're going to miss that train."

That got us moving. Marli and I were in the car in a flash, and we were on the way to the train station. We made it just in time, too.

Because we were there so late, we couldn't all sit together. Aunt Leigh and Uncle TJ sat a few rows behind us on the other side of the train. I could turn around and see them, so it was fine with me. It wasn't even fifteen minutes into the train ride before Marli was sound asleep. Thank goodness I brought my iPod for company. I looked back and saw Uncle TJ was snoozing or listening to his iPod with his eyes closed. Aunt Leigh was reading a book. She's always reading a book. She looked up and smiled at me. Yep, even with a few bad things in the last week, I have to admit that I'm pretty lucky lately.

"Keep walking. We're not going into any of these stores yet," said Uncle TJ. Marli and I were huffing along to keep up. People in Chicago sure do walk fast.

"What's the point of being on Michigan Ave if we're not shopping?" I asked as I caught up to Uncle TJ.

"We're going to let you girls do all the shopping you want, but we're starting at one end and working our way down the street. We'll go to Water Tower first. There's a ton of stores in there. You may find something perfect there, then we can just enjoy the rest of the day. If not, then we'll walk south on Michigan to see what else we see," Uncle TJ explained.

"With the mandatory stops at the Apple Store and the Disney Store," added Aunt Leigh. "And, we may just have to find Garrett's Popcorn. We haven't had that in a while."

"My mouth is watering just thinking of Chicago-style popcorn. I love it when you bring that back for us," I drooled.

"I've never had it. Must be good if you got Tay to drool," laughed Marli.

"Trust me," I nodded, "It's the best! It's caramel popcorn, buttery popcorn, and cheesy popcorn all mixed together. Yummerific!"

"Sold! I could use a snack now," teased Marli.

"You girls are always hungry," laughed Aunt Leigh. "Let's make a little detour on the way to Water Tower, hon." She smiled knowingly at Uncle TJ and he nodded back. We walked up a few more blocks and right into the Hershey's store. Yes!

"Hot cocoa or ice cream sundae. This is such a hard decision. I'm a little chilled after walking outside, but that ice cream with hot fudge looks so good too," I said. "I wish we had one of these stores closer to us, then I wouldn't have to decide. I could just have whatever I wanted more often!"

"Your aunt already makes good hot cocoa, so I'm going with the sundae," decided Marli. I followed her lead. Sounded like a good plan to me. An ice cream sundae at 10am in Chicago on a Saturday. Yep, a pretty good start to a day.

We ate fast, though, because we really wanted to get to the Water Tower. It's not a real water tower, but it is across the street from what used to be a water tower. Or something that looks like an old one at least. I'm not exactly sure. All I know is that this mall was tall and full of excellent shopping!

Now Marli and I are really great bargain shoppers. We know how to make our money work. We always start at the sales racks and are pretty good at accessorizing too. We decided to start big – Macy's – and work our way around to other stores. We agreed to meet Aunt Leigh and Uncle Carl in two hours at the Chicago store in the very top of the mall.

"Two hours in a Chicago mall – that's not enough time to even make a dent," joked Marli.

"No, our wallets don't have enough money in them to even made a dent!" I retorted.

"True that!" Marli agreed.

We headed off to Macy's to start then went to Abercrombie, Aeropostale, Forever 21, American Eagle, Hollister, and more. We tried on lots of dresses. I'll admit we looked pretty darn good in a lot of them, but all of them were way outside of our budget.

"All of these beautiful dresses…it's just not fair," complained Marli. "Do you think your aunt and uncle would give us some extra money so we can buy dresses here?"

"We are NOT going to ask them for that. They already paid for our train tickets and food here. I guess I didn't realize that Chicago is so expensive. Even the normal stores like Abercrombie seem more expensive here," I said. "Hopefully some of the other stores down Michigan Ave have big sales racks."

"Hey, there's your uncle over sitting in that comfy chair. Let's go see what's next on the plan," suggested Marli.

"Hi girls. I don't see any bags. Does that mean you didn't have any luck finding something you wanted?" asked Uncle TJ.

"Oh, we found lots we wanted…" I started.

"…but nothing we could afford," finished Marli.

"I think we might have an idea for that. Friends of ours shop at a place called Filene's Basement. It's supposed to have really nice clothing at really good deals. Aunt Leigh just went to find directions to it," offered Uncle TJ.

I was looking towards the information desk and saw Aunt Leigh talking to someone, but then my phone vibrated and distracted me. It was a text from Amber thanking me for hanging out with her last night and asking if we can schedule a time to plan for youth group activities.

"Being president is going to be all about babysitting Amber, isn't it?" I quietly asked Marli. "I like Amber, but I just don't want to be that involved."

"Just tell her you'll talk to her at youth group tomorrow. It'll all work out. She's nice enough. Just focus on shopping right now!" ordered Marli.

"Okay, it's actually just across the street. We can walk to the store. I thought it was at the other end of Michigan Avenue. Either it's been too long since I've been there or I'm really losing it," laughed Aunt Leigh. "Hopefully you girls will find something there."

We walked across Michigan Avenue to Filene's. Aunt Leigh wasn't kidding. Filene's Basement was the greatest shopping experience ever! Marli and I had so many dresses to pick from, and we could even afford to buy some jewelry to go along with them. I got this amazing midnight blue dress that only covers one shoulder and fits me like a glove. I mean, this dress literally had to have been made for me. Marli's is just as good, and the deep green really brings out her green eyes. Too bad we don't wear the same size because then we could switch dresses for spring. I can't wait for Leo to see me in this dress. I'll have to remember to tell him to get a blue tie.

"You are not going to text now," ordered Uncle TJ as he took my phone from me.

"I was just going to tell Leo about my dress," I explained. "I can't wait to see his reaction when he sees me in it, but I wanted to tell him what color it is."

"That will wait until later tonight. Right now we're going to have a little fun around Chicago. What do you girls think about taking a speedboat tour on Lake Michigan?" asked Uncle TJ.

Aunt Leigh pointed out to Lake Michigan and said, "If you've ever seen a big yellow boat speeding along…that's the Sea Dog. It's a gigantic speedboat, but they also tell you some things about Chicago. We thought it would be fun to see the city from that perspective."

"And learn something in the process," I laughed. "You know we have to learn something when we're with them, right?" I turned and looked at Marli. My aunt and uncle are fun, but they always make sure that we're learning something. I guess that makes learning interesting. "Isn't a little cold for a boat ride right now?" I'm no wimp or anything…okay, well maybe I am. I wish we were here in the summer – Chicago in the summer is so much fun.

"I didn't really dress for being outside for a long time," whined Marli.

"We weren't even thinking about that. It's probably a good point," concurred Aunt Leigh. "Any other ideas?"

"Can we go to the top of the Sears Tower? I've always wanted to do that!" I begged.

"It's not called the Sears Tower anymore, but I'm with you…it'll always be the Sears Tower to me," said Uncle TJ. "Sounds like fun. It's been years since we've gone to the top. It's a pretty clear day today, too, so we should be able to see fairly far. Should we stop somewhere to eat lunch first? I know the girls are always hungry, but I'm pretty hungry myself."

"I saw a sign for a Cheesecake Factory," suggested Marli. "I could eat mounds and mounds of cheesecake day and night!"

"Me too!" I agreed.

"It's just across the street, so it sounds good to me. Let's go eat, and then we'll walk over to the Sears Tower. There are a few more shops we can stop at along the way, and then it'll be close to time for us to get back on the train. The train stop isn't far from the Sears Tower. Good planning, Tay!" smiled Aunt Leigh.

The train ride home went by so quickly. Marli and I were just exhausted. Shopping, eating, walking, and being outside on the cold…just the right combination for a nap. We both had huge bags of Garrett's Popcorn to take home, so the train smelled so good. We had our dresses, too, and Uncle TJ bought something at the Apple Store while Aunt Leigh bought something at the Disney Store. They also bought some stuff at Crate & Barrel, but they had it shipped to their house so they didn't have to carry it on the train.

I texted Leo so he'd know when we'd be back. If the train is on time, we should get home around 9pm so I could still go out with him for a little while. I'll ask Uncle TJ if they can just drop Marli and I off at the bowling alley. I guess Marli should make sure it's okay with her mom, too. Our parents usually agree on things, but you never know.

When the train stopped in Battle Creek, I jumped up and gave Aunt Leigh and Uncle TJ each a big hug and thanked them for taking us today. "This was a way cool day. Thank you so much! We never would have found dresses like this at our mall," I sighed.

"So true," agreed Marli. "Now we just have to find the right accessories."

"You're such a diva," I laughed. "Can we just leave our stuff in your car and get it tomorrow when you come over? I really don't want to carry it around at the bowling alley. I'm not even worried about the dress, but I know Leo and his friends would eat all of our popcorn!"

Marli looked at me with horror, "I am not sharing my popcorn!"

"We'll take care of it," said Aunt Leigh. "No problems. You both can relax and just have some fun. Leo will bring you home by 11pm, right?"

"Do I need to go in and talk to Leo first?" asked Uncle TJ. He likes to try to intimidate my boyfriends, but it's always just in fun.

"I think we got it covered," I said as I punched him in the arm walking towards their car.

"Omigosh! What's that?" screeched Marli.

"What? Where are you looking?" I asked.

"Over there by the river," said Marli as she was pointing to the left. "Don't you see the big banner that has your name on it?"

"I think that's Leo standing with the lights on him," I said quite confused. "What is going on?"

"You weren't expecting this?" asked Uncle TJ.

"Obviously not, TJ, just look at her. She's completely surprised," commented Aunt Leigh. "Leo went to a lot of work to do something, so you better go check it out. Of course we're coming along, too!"

As I got closer I saw that Leo was all dressed up in khaki slacks and a polo shirt – that's really dressed up for him since he usually wears jeans with holes in them and t-shirts that should have been thrown away a long time ago. I looked around us to see if other people were around, but there weren't. There were only a few others that got off the train and they must have gone straight to their cars. What is Leo doing here?

Before I had time to ask him, Leo dropped down on one knee in front of me. "I wanted to surprise you in a very special way because I have something very special to ask you," started Leo.

"I already agreed to go to the dance with you. What's going on?" I asked.

"I love you, Tayleigh, and I always will. I've finally realized that I shouldn't wait to declare my love. I want the whole world to know how much I love you and am committed to you. Will you marry me?" Leo asked, and he seemed sincere!

Marli's mouth dropped open now too. "What did I just hear you say?" she hollered.

"Please get up, please get up, please get up," I quietly begged.

"Leo, what is all of this silliness about?" sternly asked Uncle TJ. "It's a little cold out here to be staging some theatrical show so late at night."

"It's not a show, sir, I'm serious about what I just asked," explained Leo.

"Let's all just get into the car and we can talk more about it there," suggested Aunt Leigh.

Marli jumped in, "I'll grab the banner and light." She really must have been cold to offer to do some work, or maybe she was just as eager as I was to hear Leo's explanation of what's going on.

As soon as we got into the car Leo tried to explain why he'd seriously consider proposing to me when we're only in high school, but he just sounded like a babbling idiot. I know I should think this is romantic or something, but it was just all too bizarre. I felt like I was dreaming, and I kept trying to wake myself up. I mean, I know I just wished the other day that Leo and I could be married because then we wouldn't have to worry about all of the rules of our families, but this is just ridiculous.

"Wait a minute," I yelled interrupting Leo. I turned to Marli. "Do you remember a little while ago when I wished that Leo and I could be married? Oh crap, I think I actually just thought that to myself and didn't tell you about it. Anyway, I did wish it, seriously."

Leo looked at me with wishful eyes and asked, "Does that mean your answer is yes?"

"No, no, no. Sorry Leo. We're in high school. This is all just crazy. I'm trying to figure something out here. It seems like a lot of weird things have been happening lately, and I feel like there's some pattern," I explained.

"You mean like when you wished you had your own MacBook and then you won one at school?" asked Marli.

Leo seemed to be relaxing a bit now and added, "Or when you wished I had an IV of hot cocoa and then I woke up with one in my arm the next night? Really, I swear it was there. It wasn't just a dream."

"Exactly. There has to be some pattern, don't you think?" I asked.

"Does anyone have a piece of paper and pen? We need to write these things down," suggested Aunt Leigh.

"Where do we start? Should we list what you wished for or the strange things that have happened to you?" asked Marli.

"Since you're always wishing for things, how about we write down the strange things that have happened. I can't believe that everything you've ever wished for is coming true. That's not real life," commented Aunt Leigh.

"And that's not how the snow wish is supposed to work either, is it?" added Marli. "But, just a minute…I have a recording of Tay's snow wish on my iPhone. Let's hear what she wished for. I swear it was something like all of her wishes coming true." Marli got out her iPhone and played the recording, "...I wish all of my wishes will come true!"

"Snow wishes are just for fun. It doesn't really work that way," offered Uncle TJ. "I should know, I've made hundreds of snow wishes over the years but nothing has ever come true for me. So try it out right now. Wish for something."

"I don't think it works just like that. It was earlier this week when I wished that Leo and I could be married, and he's just now asking me," I explained.

Marli chimed in, "Try one anyway!"

"Okay, okay. I wish I had a hundred dollars," I wished aloud.

"I have fifty dollars you can have," laughed Leo. "I'm sorry, but even though I asked you to marry me, I just don't believe in this whole wish thing."

"Well let's get back to this list," said Aunt Leigh. "I already wrote down that Leo asked you to marry him, you won the MacBook Pro, and the hot cocoa IV. What other odd things have happened lately?"

"We don't have any homework right now at school," quipped Marli. "That's one of the most bizarre things to happen to us ever, and I wish it was forever!"

"I did wish for no more homework so we'd have more time to do other things," I replied.

“What about Bryant going to college early? I’ve never heard of a program like that,” said Leo.

“I wished I could have his room now because I wanted a bigger bedroom, and I knew that wasn’t going to happen until he left for college,” I countered.

“This is getting a little freaky,” cried Marli. “Are all of your wishes really coming true?”

“I wish stuff all of the time, so there’s no way I’d ever be able to figure that out. I’m sure there’s some wishes that haven’t come true,” I suggested.

“I know one!” shouted Marli. “You wished that Alex would leave you alone when he kept pestering you about your jeans. He didn’t leave you alone and even got you in trouble when he gave you the answers for the test.”

“That’s right, and I definitely did wish that. And, that was after we made the snow wish. Okay, none of this is making sense now,” I sighed.

“Singing. That’s another unusual thing on the list. I always believed in you, but you never believed in yourself that you could sing so well. And look at it now – you’re singing a solo in the choir concert and another one in front of the band,” said Aunt Leigh.

"What about the weird way that Polly and Jason have been acting lately? They're almost like zombies at times. Did you wish for anything dealing with them?" asked Uncle TJ.

"I did. I totally forgot about that. I wished they weren't so competitive all of the time. But I think I wished for that before my snow wish. Come to think of it, I'm pretty sure I wished about marrying Leo before the snow wish. I think it was that morning. Leo, Marli, and I came over to your house after school," I remembered as I looked at Aunt Leigh and Uncle TJ, "but I'd already made some of these wishes earlier that day."

"Let's listen to that wish again, Marli," proposed Uncle TJ. "This time play the whole recording. We need to listen to every single word."

Marli turned up the volume on her iPhone and played my wish:

I know what I'll wish for – it'll be the wish to top all wishes today.
I wish all of my wishes will come true!

"You were speaking a little dramatically there," commented Aunt Leigh. "Some very dramatic pauses."

"Marli was being overly dramatic when she did her wish, so I was making fun of her a little bit," I admitted as I smiled at Marli. She just giggled.

"If you listen to the pauses, it almost sounds like 'Today I wish all of my wishes will come true…' meaning that the wishes you wished on that day would come true, not all of your wishes," clarified Uncle TJ.

"Omigosh! You're absolutely right! That would explain why my other wishes haven't come true," I exclaimed. "And you know that with as many wishes as I make in a day, there could be dozens of wishes I made that day. Small ones like being in band to big ones like getting married."

"We'll never be able to figure out all of the wishes you made and what happened with them," said Marli.

"Does this mean we're not getting married?" asked Leo.

We all looked at him and laughed.

"I think it's a little too late to think on this any more tonight, and we're not going to change anything yet tonight. Let's talk more tomorrow after church when we're all at Tayleigh's house," suggested Aunt Leigh.

"That's if I sleep at all tonight! I don't think I'll be able to turn off the thinking until I get this all figured out," I complained.

"That means I'm coming over too to be part of this," quipped Marli.

"Me too," added Leo. "I'm so confused right now." We all laughed again. But he's right, I'm so confused too!

By the time I got home, we already had a list of ten wishes I had made that day…or at least that we think I'd made that day. We're calling it The Snow Wish List…catchy name, isn't it? Here's what I have so far:

1. *Hot cocoa IV for Leo*
2. *Married to Leo now*
3. *My own MacBook Pro*
4. *No homework*
5. *A bigger room (meaning Bryant goes to college early)*
6. *Singing like Miley Cyrus*
7. *Less competition between Polly & Jason*
8. *Cafeteria at school open all of the time*
9. *Everyone would love my outfits*
10. *Drive-thru restaurant that serves everything*

I know ten wishes seem like a lot, but I'm sure there were more. I wish for things all of the time. Call me a dreamer, I don't care. I wish I could remember all of my wishes. Wait, I don't really mean that. You know, it's fun to wish for things, but now I think I'm going to be a little more careful about my wishes. What if Leo didn't wake up with his arm feeling warm – that IV of hot cocoa could have really hurt him! I think I need to figure out how to fix a few of my wishes.

Some didn't hurt anyone, but some are making a big difference. I've never been that good of a singer, and all of a sudden I'm just phenomenal. Is that fair? Will it last? Should someone else be singing the choir solo or with the band? What if I get up there to sing and my voice turns back to normal? What about Bryant…is he really ready to go to college? I know my mom is going to miss him so much. Should he stay home another semester? And then there's Polly and Jason…things just aren't right with them. They've lost a lot of their excitement about life. I guess the fighting and competition was part of that excitement, and they're kind of boring without it.

Aunt Leigh and Uncle TJ explained to me that I couldn't rely on a wish to fix it all. I was thinking I could make another snow wish, and then everything would go back to normal. But, I have been making snow wishes my whole life, and this is the first one that actually came true. I guess it's unrealistic to think I can wish all of the changes away. It sure would be easier, though.

I quickly explained everything to my parents, and I'm asking them to help me figure out what to do. Isn't that what parents are there for? To help you out when you've made a mess of things? I sure hope so…

"This all sounds very bizarre, but let's follow your line of thinking. I think you need to start by making a list of each of your wishes," suggested Mom.

"We did that in the car at the train station and on the way home. We have ten wishes on the list," I replied.

"Are you sure that's all of them? You want to make sure you're able to make everything right that you can," pushed Dad.

"I'll keep thinking. I'll have Marli and Leo help me some more since they're with me most of the time. The hard thing is that some of the wishes were just in my head, so it means I have to remember them," I explained. "But, the more I think about things, the more I seem to remember. Like I just remembered that I wished Leo could pick me up at home on the way to school, and you guys magically changed your mind and let him start picking me up."

"Thankfully not all of your wishes have negative consequences," said Mom. "We would have eventually agreed to Leo taking you to school."

"But some of your wishes are having a lasting impact, and you need to think about those carefully," cautioned Dad. "With your wish list, you need to list what has actually happened and if anyone has been hurt in the process. Seriously think about the impact of each wish."

"Let's look at one together," Mom offered. "Look at number eight – the cafeteria at school being open more often."

"Everyone is happy about that one," I smiled. "We can get snacks before school and in between classes. It's been great!"

"Did you think about Mrs. Appleton, the cafeteria worker? How is being open all of these hours affecting her? Is she working too much now? Is she getting paid for the extra hours? You have to think about all angles – not just how it makes your friends' lives easier," explained Dad.

I thought for a minute. "Wow, I never even thought of Mrs. Appleton. I'll have to ask her how it's going having the cafeteria open more hours. And, if it's too much for her, then maybe I can organize a group of students or start a petition to make sure she gets the help she needs or the school decreases the hours the café is open." Wow, that felt good. I'm making plans. I can do things without wishes. "You guys are right. I'll start working on a plan to make things right wherever I can. Some things are already fixed like numbers one and two. Leo doesn't have a hot cocoa IV anymore, and I'm definitely not marrying him now!"

"You certainly aren't, young lady!" sternly warned Dad.

"Calm down, honey, she's doing the right things. I think she's learned quite a lesson about wishing, too. You never know when things may come true, so you want to think it out. That lesson applies to more than just wishes. You need to know where you want to go in life and how to get there, but always consider what happens along the way and make sure you don't hurt anyone intentionally or unintentionally. And, if someone does get hurt, you do what you can to make it right," lectured Mom. "That's lecture number 923."

I chuckled. Mom always numbers her lectures when she's being kind of silly. If it's a really stern lecture, then it doesn't get a number. I definitely like the numbered lectures better!

CHAPTER 7

Sunday after church Marli, Leo, Aunt Leigh, and Uncle TJ all came over so we could brainstorm about what to do with this Snow Wish List. Of course my parents were there to help. Jason and Bryant were even going to try to help, although Jason didn't really seem too interested in it. Hopefully they can all help me figure out if I've missed anything, too.

"There's some of these wishes that you can't do anything about," said Marli. "They're just happening and we don't have anything to do with it. Like homework. We have to start homework again after Christmas break, so it's not like homework was eliminated forever."

"I agree with Marli," said Leo. "Wow, I'm agreeing with her too much lately!" We all laughed. "You can't do anything about people liking your outfits. It's not like you can make a general announcement to everyone to stop liking your outfits – that would just be strange. I think we take both of those wishes off the list."

"I could spread a rumor about Tay's clothes that would make everyone start hating whatever she's wearing," snickered Bryant.

"Not helping, Bry," chuckled Dad as he pretended to reprimand him.

"I'll ignore the peanut gallery. Okay, if we remove those two from the list, then there's less work that needs to be done to try to fix things," I replied. "I'm already exhausted just spending time last night trying to think of things to fix. That reminds me, you're not going to ask me to marry you again, are you Leo?"

"Nope. I think I'm thinking straight now," Leo answered.

"Hallelujah for that!" shouted Marli. "I mean, I would have loved to be the maid of honor, but it's all a little crazy to think about."

"Agreed!" Leo and I said at the same time. He leaned over and gave me a quick peck on the cheek. "I still love you, though," said Leo. "You're not getting rid of me that easily."

"I kind of want you to stay around," I smiled.

"We may have just learned something here," commented Aunt Leigh. "Tay wished that she was married to Leo, so he asked her to marry him. But, he came to his senses. So, it's not like these wishes are forever or they have to come true. It sounds like common sense still has some power."

"Common sense should always win out, but it's usually missing when it comes to teenagers!" laughed Uncle TJ. "That's a good observation, though. The answer to some of the wishes may be just to talk to people to make some changes."

"Well let's get back to the list, then, and see," I suggested. "I'm going to go talk to Mrs. Kipp tomorrow to make sure that the MacBook Pro really should be mine. I want to make sure the way that she drew the names out was fair. I realize the wish made it happen, but if she thinks it was still all fair…I mean, my name could have been drawn out anyway, right?"

"Your mom would probably tell you to give the MacBook Pro back and ask Mrs. Kipp to draw out someone else's name, but I think you're right. You could have won that computer anyway. I like your plan," concurred Marli as she looked to the right at my mom.

"I actually agree with you, too," said Mom. "You didn't force Mrs. Kipp to draw your name and there were other names who got drawn as well. You had the same chance as everyone else. I think you can cross this one off of your list too. It may have been because of the wish, but it may have just been some good luck."

Uncle TJ smiled but didn't say anything. He sure does love Macs. I'm sure he was quietly doing a cheerleader kick in his mind.

"What about Bryant's college program? Are you going to call the University of Michigan and see if he really should be in the program?" asked Leo.

"I don't think I should do anything about that one either. It is a new program at U of M. Mom and Dad checked into it – it's real.

Besides, Bryant's grades are perfect. I think he would have been admitted to this program even without my wish. I don't want to be the reason it gets taken away from him. I think that would do more harm," I stated.

Bryant nodded, "I'd like to think I got in to the program on my own merit. It was a little unusual that there were multiple students from our area that got admitted into the program, but hopefully it was because we all deserve it."

"You do deserve it, Bryant. I'm going to miss you like crazy, but I know the hard adjusting is more on my part than on yours. It's always hard when a baby leaves the nest," said Mom, as she got a little teary-eyed.

"I'm not a baby," whined Bryant.

"I know. I know. Just bear with me a little bit," explained Mom as she gave Bryant a hug.

Dad walked over and hugged Bryant too. "We are so proud of you, son. I have no doubt you got into that program based on your own good work, and I know you will excel once you are there."

"Whew! That's good," said Leo. "I didn't want to be around Bryant if that got taken away from him. He's been wearing his Michigan jerseys nonstop ever since he got accepted into that program. I know he's really looking forward to it."

I saw Mom and Dad look at each other while we were talking. Not sure what that look meant, but hopefully they still think we're doing everything right.

"We can't do anything about the drive-thru restaurant either. It's not like we can close down the restaurant," asserted Marli.

"Aunt Leigh said that restaurant has been a huge success. I guess there was an article in the newspaper saying they might open one on the other side of town, too. I think that wish actually did something good. People always want something that's more convenient, and going to one drive-thru instead of several makes life much easier," I clarified.

"Starting a new business in this economy is very scary, so it's even more impressive that they're considering opening another one. But let's be realistic, there's no way your wish magically caused that restaurant to open overnight. I think it was all about timing. You can throw together a menu, staffing, and a location in one night. I think it just happened at the same time you made the wish," explained Uncle TJ.

Dad nodded his head and said, "I agree. It's a little bizarre that you thought of it and it happened, but it must have already been planned. I don't think you need to worry about that one."

"This list is getting easier as we go along. It feels much more manageable to me now," said Leo.

"I'm so glad all of you are here to help me with things," I said as I hugged Leo and Marli who were closest to me. "It's good to have such good friends and family that I can count on when I need it."

"I always have your back," said Marli as she gave me an extra squeeze.

"What do you guys think about the singing? I've never been this good at singing. I have no idea how long it'll last. What if I get up there at the choir concert or band concert then can't sing?" I asked. I know that sounds selfish, but I'm really worried about that. I'd be totally humiliated. I'm already nervous enough about being in front of everyone, but now I have to worry about if the wish is permanent or not.

"So what are you saying? Are you going to back out?" asked Leo. "I'd miss seeing you at band practice."

"Wait, that reminds me, this is really two wishes. I wished I could sing like Miley Cyrus, and I wished I could be in band with you guys. I just realized that!" I exclaimed.

"That doesn't change what Leo asked," pushed Dad. "Are you backing out of singing the solos? If you do, how are you going to explain that to Ms. Planter and Mr. Shets?"

"I don't know. I really don't think it's fair. Someone else would have been selected to do both solos. I mean, I love it now that I've gotten used to the idea, but I guess I should go talk to Ms. Planter and Mr. Shets," I sadly said. I didn't think I'd like singing the solos. I was so nervous to begin with, but I found that I really liked doing it. And I was good. Or, at least the wish made me good. UGH! I hate this. I don't even know what is real anymore.

"What are you going to say to your teachers, though? It's not like you can explain to them that you were chosen because of a wish," pondered Uncle TJ.

I sighed. I have no clue. Why can't I wish my way out of this? I looked around at everyone and pleaded, "I'm open to any suggestions. I really have no idea."

"What about asking your teachers if they had someone else on the list as a back-up in case you got sick, then you'd know who they may have used otherwise. You know the kids in choir, so you'd be able to tell if that person is someone who normally would have sung the solos," offered Aunt Leigh.

Marli jumped in, "Or you can just tell them you're feeling sick, then they'll have to get someone else. Then you don't have to worry about the wish wearing off or anything."

"I think Mr. Shets would have picked you anyway. He thought it was cool that you and I are dating and would have solos together in the song," said Leo.

"Didn't you say Ms. Planter was trying to spread solos around more within the choir? Maybe it was just your turn," said Mom.

I thought on that for a minute. "She did ask me to sing before she even heard me sing like Miley Cyrus. She asked me to sing it because of the song," I explained. "Maybe you're both right. Maybe I really would be singing both solos. I want to do them. I really do. I just want it to be fair."

"I think you should sing both solos and do your best at them. But, if you're asked to do another solo in the near future, I think you should make sure someone else gets a chance," suggested Uncle TJ.

"I can live with that idea…as long as my voice holds out," I agreed.

Marli slapped me upside the head as she said, "You have a good voice even without your wish. I think the wish just gave you more confidence to be able to sing like we all knew you could. Even if that wish goes away, you'll still do a great job singing."

Aren't best friends the best? She knows when to hug me and she knows when to slap me!

"I guess we're down to the last wish. How do I get Polly and Jason to be normal again?" I asked everyone.

"Ya, it's just too freaky how they agree on everything now. It's like their personality got sucked out of them," commented Marli.

Jason looked half asleep on the couch. "I still have a personality," he quietly said. "I just feel like I was too rushed about everything and always trying to win. I realized that I can slow down a bit, and that's okay with me."

"That's just weird," laughed Marli, "and so not you!"

"I agree that a little less competition between Jason and Polly would be fine, but it seems that without competition they don't have any drive to do just about anything," said Mom. "I had to force Polly to go to Allie's house this weekend, and you know how she is normally begging to go there."

Uncle TJ winked at me as he said, "I can understand Jason's point of view. He probably was sick of Polly beating him at everything. It's a lot easier to just give up on competition in general rather than losing all of the time."

I immediately understood what he was doing and added, "You're right. I hadn't realized it before. It does seem like Polly won more often than Jason. You know, getting to sit in the front seat, eating the last piece of bacon, getting the A+ on an assignment at school, memorizing a poem first…I could go on and on."

"Maybe if Jason doesn't think he can beat Polly at anything, I should try. It's hardly fair for a senior to compete with a 5th grader, but I think it could be fun," joined in Bryant.

"I never said Polly was better than me!" exclaimed Jason as he sat up straight on the couch. "I'm not giving up because she always win. I win a lot of the time, probably even more often than she does." I could see the old fire starting to ignite in his eyes.

"You don't have to defend yourself, Jason, we understand," commiserated Aunt Leigh. "If I had a twin that was smarter, faster, and more popular than I was, I'd have a hard time with it too."

We were all trying so hard not to crack up. Mom and Dad didn't join in the jabbing, probably because they would have laughed if they tried to say anything. Jason looked like he was ready to explode.

"You guys are all so stupid! I'll show you who's smarter, faster, and more popular! Just wait and see!" Jason yelled as he stormed up to his room.

"Risky, but well played," laughed Dad as soon as Jason was upstairs. We all laughed quietly so Jason couldn't hear us.

"Should we try the same type of thing with Polly?" I asked.

"I think unleashing Jason may be just the thing to bring our Polly back as well," Mom answered. "If Jason starts getting competitive again, I can't imagine Polly just standing idly by and ignoring him. Let's give it a day or two and see what happens."

"Thank you! Thank you! Thank you!" I shouted as I ran around the room hugging everyone. "Yesterday I thought my wishes would be the end of me, but all of you helped me see that it's not as bad as I thought it would be. I still have some things I need to fix, but the world isn't ending."

"Um…not sure how to say this, Tay, but I think there's another wish we missed," said Marli quite somberly.

"I'm sure there's lot of wishes we missed, but I feel like we got all of the big ones," I replied.

"What about Alex?" asked Marli.

"What about him?" retorted Leo. "We already had him on the list, then we took him off. Tay wished he would stop bugging her, but that was after the snow wish day. That wish didn't take effect."

"I think you must have wished something that caused him to give you the answers to the math quiz, which is why he got suspended from school," suggested Marli. "That's it – answers! Didn't you wish for something like all of the answers?"

"Holy cow, you're right! When I was rambling all of the wishes that day when we were doing homework, one of them was something about having all of the answers. That's exactly what Alex gave me – all of the answers to the math quiz," I said as I sagged down into the couch that Jason just left. I felt as low as he looked a few minutes ago. It was all my fault that Alex got suspended from school. He was just trying to be nice to me. It wasn't anything to do with Vanessa at all!

"I've never known Alex to cheat before, so I don't think this was typical behavior for him," added Leo.

"The whole incident didn't go on my permanent record because I turned in Alex and I didn't even use the answer key, but it probably did go on Alex's record," I said.

"Plus everyone thinks he's a cheater now," stated Marli. "His reputation is really hurting. And personally, I think he's really pretty great."

"Thanks. You're making me feel so much better," I said as I sunk down even deeper into the couch.

Aunt Leigh came over and sat down by me, putting her arm around me as she said, "You're not to blame in this, Tayleigh. You didn't wish for Alex to cheat or for him to be suspended from school. Your wish just manifested itself in a way that you didn't expect."

"Which I why I said earlier that we have to be careful what we wish for," interrupted Mom.

Aunt Leigh nodded, "It's true. Wishes, plans, or actions – we need to think about the consequences of what we do. You know that, though. This was unintentional. I don't necessarily see any way to explain to the principal or your math teacher what the situation really is, but there are other things you could do to help Alex move forward."

"You could find out if there's any way to expunge his permanent record. For example, the school may have a policy that if you do so many hours of community service, you can have a suspension removed after it's already been served," suggested Uncle TJ.

"Or you can offer to help Alex with homework or tutoring in a subject that he might be struggling in," recommended Dad.

"Or you can just be his friend," added Mom. "You said before that you wished he'd stop bugging you. Well, we know he was bugging you because you wished everyone would love your outfit, so that wasn't really his fault either. It seems that Alex has gotten a raw deal with your wishes, so maybe the way you can make it up to him is to be his friend."

"I think all of your ideas sound good. I'm going to do them all," I stated.

"He should be back in school tomorrow, and I'll help you. I kind of feel like I'm partially responsible for all of this because you were with me when we were randomly shouting out all kinds of wishes that day," offered Marli.

"I appreciate that, but you're off the hook. It's all me, but I'll still take you up on your offer to help. Maybe we can see if Alex and his date…if he has one…want to go to the dance in a group with all of us." I thought out loud.

"Actually, you might want to take that back," laughed Leo. "I heard that Vanessa asked Alex to go with her!"

"No way!" shouted Marli. "I'm not spending an evening with that witch! It's not fair, I was kind of thinking of asking Alex to go with me."

My parents, aunt, and uncle all started to open their mouths at once, but I jumped in and said, "I think we've learned from this little adventure that everyone can be misunderstood…from wishes to witches." That was clever…I crack myself up sometimes. "Even if Alex is going to the dance with Vanessa, I think we should still do it. We'll make the best of it. Who knows, maybe Vanessa will learn that we're actually good people and stop being so evil to us all of the time. But, Marli, why don't you text him and see if he has a date…"

"I feel a little forward in doing that," sheepishly said Marli.

"I'll ask him – guy to guy," said Leo. Leo went ahead and texted Alex to see what was going on with him. Alex said he was nervous about going back to school, worried about how kids would treat him. He also told Vanessa he didn't want to go to the dance with her, which made Marli smile. Leo suggested he ask Marli to the dance, and Alex said he'd think about it.

"Maybe I'll even talk to y'all at the dance, although that would cramp my style a bit," laughed Bryant. "It probably would elevate Alex's status to have a senior talking to him, though. Ya, I can do that."

"Your father and I are so proud of all of you. It takes a very special person to want to right any wrongs that have been done, and it takes a special group of friends and family to be supportive," said Mom. Uh-oh, she's getting teary-eyed again. Maybe I'll have to get her a giant box of Kleenex for Christmas.

"We're so proud of you, too, Tayleigh," continued Aunt Leigh. "If we'd had a daughter, I wish she would have been just like you…"

I jumped up and put my hand over Aunt Leigh's mouth while laughing, "Stop! No more wishes for a while! I can't handle it!"

CHAPTER 8

I thought about wishes all last night. How could I not? I wonder if it really was my wishes that made these things happen or if it was all just a big coincidence? It seems like a lot of the things really could have happened on their own, but the timing of all of it was very strange. I just can't imagine that making a snow wish really works. All of the snow wishes everyone in my family has ever made, and none of them have come true until now.

I guess I sat in my room thinking a little too long because Mom yelled up to me telling me I was running late. I hurried downstairs to grab some breakfast, or what was left of it. The pancakes and bacon were all gone, so I had to settle for some fruit.

"I guess I'm way too late since all of the food is gone," I sighed.

"Actually, the twins pigged everything down. Polly finished the last pancake and Jason grabbed the last piece of bacon," smiled Bryant. "I think they're back to normal."

"Oh, that's awesome!" I squealed. I never thought I'd be excited about competition between the twins. Wait a minute…Polly and Jason…middle school. Oh no!

"Mom, I just thought of another wish!" I yelled. She came into the kitchen from the living room. "I wished that the twins wouldn't have to go to the same middle school I did, and now they're going to a special middle school. What do we need to do about that? I really want them to go to the new school."

Mom smiled, "I didn't realize you'd made a wish on that one, too, but don't worry about it. When I met with their teacher, he'd already met with a few other families and we were the last ones he told. I'm pretty sure this was all set in motion before your wish."

"As was another thing we were talking about," interrupted Dad. He nodded at Mom. "I just got off the phone with the University of Michigan admissions office, just so we could confirm everything and not worry about it." He turned and looked at Bryant. "You can be assured that you got into the program because of your own merit, not a wish. The approval list for early admissions was signed by the Board the previous Friday, but it was too late in the day to notify anyone so they waited until first thing Monday morning."

Bryant did a fist pump in the air with a big smile on his face.

"I never doubted it for a minute," said Mom. "We're always so proud of you, Bry."

"Thanks, Mom. Thanks, Dad," Bryant said as he hugged them both.

I'm so glad both of these situations worked out. I would have felt awful if anything I'd done hurt any of my siblings. Was that just a horn I heard?

"You better get going," said Dad. "Leo is here."

"You're still letting him pick me up? You guys rock!" I exclaimed as I quickly kissed each of my parents on the cheek.

I grabbed my computer and coat and ran out to the car to explain what had happened this morning with Bryant and the twins. It was starting out to be a good day. Leo leaned over to give me a big kiss, and I backed away a bit turned to see if my parents were watching.

"What's wrong?" asked Leo.

"I just remembered another wish. I wished something about wanting us to be like other couples who aren't afraid to express their love in public. Maybe that's why Marli keeps teasing us for kissing so much in public lately," I explained.

"Not that I mind at all," laughed Leo. "But I really don't need gawkers. If you want to dial it back a bit in public, I'm fine with that. I still get to hold your hand, right?"

"Of course. And you better still kiss me now!" I said as I threw my arms around his neck. Definitely a good start to the day.

"Again? You're at it again?" yelled Marli as she rushed up to the car and opened the door to get in the back seat.

"That display was only for you," I joked. Now I have to explain all of the morning's happenings all over again to Marli.

After I finished doing that and we were almost to school, Marli announced, "I'm going to ask Alex to the dance today. I'm not going to wait for him to ask me. I'm just going to do it. That way I feel like I'm doing something to help out, too. Or, at least I can justify doing it if I explain it to myself that way. I really want to go with him, but I'd be too nervous to ask him otherwise. So, please tell me that I'm really helping if I ask him to go."

"You are. It's very helpful. I feel just horrible about what happened with Alex, it's probably the worst thing that did happen. I'd love for him to go to the dance with us so I can try to make it up to him as well. And, if you're happy in the process, all the better," I shared.

Leo nudged me and said, "Marli, you better get your words ready because there he is." Alex was walking along the sidewalk heading to Leo's car, which was in the opposite direction of the school.

"Hi guys," Alex shouted as he waved.

"Oh Alex, I'm so, so sorry," I started.

“Stop right there, Tayleigh. It’s not your fault. What I did was wrong. I’m not sure why I thought giving you the quiz answers was going to help with anything. I really don’t know why I did that, but it was my fault. I don’t blame you at all. I’m sorry you got in trouble, too. I should have listened to you when you said you didn’t want the answers. You’re off the dance team, and I’m sorry for that,” explained Alex.

I walked over to him and gave him a quick, awkward hug. “I guess we’re both sorry. I promise next time you ask me something, like about my clothes or anything, I’ll give you a straight answer. I thought you were in cahoots with Vanessa, and anything to do with her bugs me,” I laughed.

“She can be nice once in a while, but I totally understand,” smiled Alex. “Hey Marli, I have a quick question to ask you.”

Marli brightened up right away. I could tell she was holding her breath.

Alex continued, “I know the dance is this week, so I’m really late in asking this, but I was wondering…”

“Yes! Yes! Yes!” Marli screeched.

“You will? You don’t have any plans for the dance already?” Alex asked with a big smile on his face.

“I do have plans, and now you do too. We’ll go to the dance with Tay and Leo. It’s going to be great! My dress is green, so we’ll have to make sure you have a green tie. I'm thinking I'd like to go to Olive Garden for dinner, but we have time to figure that out..." Marli continued as she hooked her arm into Alex's arm and started dragging him off towards the school.

Leo and I just laughed at them, especially at the look of complete confusion yet total happiness on Alex's face. His life has just been taken over by the Marli monster. He won't know what hit him. But, it's wonderful, we're going to have a great time at the dance.

I wish every Monday started this well…

The Author

Wendy is an avid reader and likes to encourage children to read. She wrote *The Snow Wish* as a way to inspire her nieces to read. She hopes it encourages other kids to start reading and dreaming. Wendy plans to write several more books in the Wish series, including her next book called *The Jefferson Wish*. Wendy lives in Michigan with her husband, Paul, and their two cats, Polly and Plato.

You can visit Wendy's web site at
www.wendytackett.com
or become a fan of The Snow Wish at
www.facebook.com/thesnowwish